Echoes of Gasping Souls

Gurucharan Singh Gandhi

Leadstart

ISBN: 978-81-948043-5-2

Cover design: Mihir Joglekar
Layout: Kshitij Dhawale, Leadstart
Printing: Jasmine Printers

Published in India 2021 by
Leadstart
A Division of One Point Six Technologies Pvt Ltd
Building J2, Shram Seva Premises, Offices: 119-123
Wadala Truck Terminus, Wadala (East)
Mumbai 400 037, Maharashtra, INDIA
T + 91 96 99933000 **E** info@leadstartcorp.com
W www.leadstartcorp.com

Gurdip Singh Gandhi
I owe my voice and my words to you.

Gagan
Thank you for serving Dad when it mattered the most.

Rohit Jain
For taking care of my family when I could not be there.

∽ CONTENTS ∼

ABOUT THE AUTHOR

Gurucharan Singh Gandhi, in his own words, is a 'full time corporate *wallah* and a part time writer'.

His debut book 'Kabeer in Korporates' published in 2016, in English and thereafter translated to Hindi and Marathi, was a national bestseller and won the *'Best Debut Manuscript* in Non-Fiction' at 'Lit-O-Fest'.

Born and raised in Jhinkpani, a dusty hamlet in Jharkhand, his writings have the sensibility of small-town India coupled with its inescapable complexes.

Prologue

'Sunil Paswan is dead' – he wrote on the WhatsApp group. 'He died yesterday.'

'What!', 'Oh shit', 'Are you sure?' – were the responses from the other three members in the group within a few minutes. He was still staring at the screen in a daze, not knowing what to write back. He was grappling with grief at the news. There was silence on the screen, but a tempest raged in his mind. He also knew that each member in the group was going through the same.

Dying is an extremely personal thing – only the person concerned dies. Those who are emotionally wedded to the deceased feel that their world will no longer remain the same, but the truth of life is also that it goes on. This death, however, was different. Even in death Sunil Paswan had proved that he was superior to them. We might survive the biggest scares but will succumb to the meanest streak of a fellow human being's soul. This news was the beginning of what was perhaps was the worst nightmare for all of them – the nightmare of the soul – as if all those days that they had survived together were not nightmarish enough!

Since yesterday he was seeing his home in an altogether different way. He had noticed things that he had not noticed in a long time. He had noticed that the photograph of his wedding reception was now almost two decades old and that he looked very awkward and conscious standing with his newly wedded wife. He noticed that there was a pen stand that was on the side stand, the one that he had bought for his son when he was in class 8. He noticed that his wife had a few more wrinkles on her face than the last time he remembered. He also noticed that he did not remember when the curtains and upholstery were changed. Since the time he had returned from Mumbai he had started to notice these things and many more. Meeting death makes you alive to the tiniest details – it makes you realise how precious they are.

The news of Sunil Paswan's death shattered him. He felt the room closing in on him. There was a loud noise between his ears – he was not able to think or hear a thing. He felt a tight lump in his heart building up. Even breathing was an effort. The reason for his death only made him angry.

'What did Sunil's death mean for him?' – he did not even want to think about it. However, he knew he had to think about it. The others had to think about it too – Kulwant Kaur, with her lovely salt and pepper hair and caring personality had to think about it, Razia Sheikh with her large 'Mallu' eyes and mature outlook had to think about it, Manoj Joshi with his big intellect and loud mouth had to think of it, and he, Sitam Pradhan in his flat in Lutyens Delhi with a new newfound sensibility had to think about it.

Sunil Paswan could not think because he was dead. He would have wished that he had died of the COVID-19 like a million others but he was not lucky enough. He had escaped from the worst and the most diabolic human instinct 30 years ago in his village in Bihar, little knowing that it would catch up with him in Mumbai.

Everyone had to think about it for a very simple reason – they had stayed together in the same hotel in suburban Mumbai during the lockdown for the first 21 days and then beyond, first out of compulsion and thereafter out of choice.

'Damn the world!' Sitam muttered in anger.

PART 1

1. Day Zero

It was a normal day, as normal as it could be given the storms that were brewing across the world. The trouble with bad times is that first they happen slowly around us, leading us to believe that it is happening only to others, and that somehow it will leave us untouched – then all of a sudden it explodes on us!

Hotel Landmark and its manager Sunil Paswan were both veterans in the business of dealing with guests. The hotel had seen better times but now it was running on the twin engines of familiarity and comfort. Old timers were too used to the hotel and it was conveniently near the airport. These two factors often took away the attention of the patrons from a rather average upkeep and a complete lack of fancy facilities that hotels these days are known for.

Hotel Landmark had middle-class written all over it. Sunil Paswan was just the perfect manager for such a hotel – a middle-class manager for a middle-class hotel.

He had joined the hotel as the doorman around the time it had opened its doors to guests thirty years ago and had grown to become its manager. His journey was made sweetest the day he was called a 'manager' because that was something beyond his wildest imagination, a far cry from the tumultuous circumstances under which he had to flee his village in the district Ara in Bihar, right after his schooling, when he was only 16-years-old.

Only in a hotel like Landmark could someone like a Sunil Paswan become a manager. He was forty-seven now but looked older. Life has a funny way of showing up on your face.

It was not a busy day. The number of guests over the last few days had dwindled significantly with all the furore about the Coronavirus flowing thick and fast. In fact, only four rooms were occupied as of now. Mr Paswan was worried.

Mumbai was cautious but still going about its business as best as it could, given its propensity to be in a perpetual state of business-as-usual. It had not stopped for riots, floods, bombs and rains and it was unlikely that it would come to a standstill for something as tiny as a virus.

Sunil had been reading about the Coronavirus spread with amusement. He understood serious problems like bombs and riots, but he just could not fathom how people could be afraid of a disease which according to him was nothing more than mere cough and cold.

'These are fears of the rich. It's a disease of the rich,' he said aloud from behind his newspaper. Cholera is serious, malaria is serious, TB is serious. This is just some cough and fever,' he muttered under his breath, as if he were still in his village in the backyard of Bihar.

There was a part of him that had still not been able to adjust to the joys and fears of this city. The truth is that a village sees sickness and its seriousness differently; the violence of nature is dealt with poise and equanimity – there is no reason to panic if it's the fury of nature. Its karma, some kind of tax paid to the Gods. Its fury is secular – everyone, irrespective of your name or caste or status was equally susceptible. There was spiritual relief in that.

Panic happens when it is man-made. Caste violence and the killings of the Maoists that he had grown with, were things to be really worried about. One worried about them because one would be a victim of its fury because your name was Sunil Paswan. Names in villages are more than mere names. They have castes written all over them. He realised he had allowed his mind to wander.

As he saw a wave of humanity moving about outside, his mind moved to the Prime Minister's address that was due to begin in some time. He smiled at all the memes that he had read since morning – the memories of the PM addressing the nation at night had become the source of hundreds of jokes and memes. 'Mitron' – he uttered the word in his mind and started to smile. He increased the volume of the TV above as he sat on the counter of Hotel Landmark in the city of Mumbai.

"Mere pyare deshwasiyo....' The PM began... '....corona mahamari se bachne ka ekmatr vikalp hai...social distancing...desh aaj ek mahatvapurn nirnay karne ja raha hai...aaj raat 12 baje se sampurn desh me sampurn lockdown hone jaa raha hai.....hindustan ko bachane ke liye gharo se bahar nikalne se poori pabandi lagai ja rahi hai...lockdown kia ja raha hai...for 21 days...till.. "

"My countrymen, there is only one solution to dealing with the Coronavirus spread, that is social distancing...the country is taking the decision of going going under complete lockdown from today midnight...this is the only way to save the country...this will last for 21 days."

It took some time for Sunil Paswan to register what he was hearing. He was too numb to understand what this implied.

∞◇∞

Kulwant Kaur was enjoying the sights of the Gateway through her touristy eyes. It was her first trip to Mumbai – actually, it was her first trip anywhere alone. Dressed in classical Patiala salwar, with liberal salt and pepper in her long hair, more salt than pepper, she was the quintessential Punjabi woman at sixty-two-years – graceful and difficult to ignore.

She was enjoying the wide sight of the sea in front of her, and the helpless bobbling of the boats on the waves reminded her of herself – for all her life she she had been a boat at the mercy of the waves. The boats were out in the sea and free to be what they wanted to be, yet they looked so helpless as they floated there, bobbling up and down, giving the impression of being free but not really being so. Only she knew how it felt to have merely a notion of freedom.

This whole trip for her was about the boat being finally free.

She looked around and enjoyed being free amidst so much of activity. They told her that the madness was actually far less today. She cursed the Corona scare in her mind. She could see the majestic Taj hotel on the other side, something she had only seen on TV. She spent the next few hours on the sea face. It was beyond 8 in the evening and the lights had come out.

Her phone rang. It was her husband. 'There has been a lockdown announced by the PM today – you cannot move out for the next 21 days.' She could hear the concern and anger in his voice. Her trip had become a cause for bitterness between them. The whole idea of going on a solo trip at this age was something he did not quite understand. It was not a question of whether he approved of it or not – because approval was neither sought nor discussed; it was about whether it was a sensible thing to do. One fine day, Kulwant had announced her plans to go for a solo trip, covering the gurudwaras in Bidar, Karnataka and Nanded in Maharashtra and the birthplace of Namdeo in Pandharpur – the religiosity was a smart wrapper for her first solo trip. In India one can argue with law, logic and even emotion – but no one messes with the Gods.

She had been pressured to return a few days earlier, but she had not relented saying she would return by train to Delhi and then to Amritsar, her hometown in a few days. 'Now this lockdown!' she cursed. She hurried to her hotel – Hotel Landmark.

Sitam Pradhan in his mid-forties was like any other bureaucrat who is stuck in the Indian bureaucracy – extremely bright but bored, well-read but frustrated, intelligent but useless.

He was right now sitting in one of those government offices which are notorious for being cramped, dirty and grossly incompetent. Every inch of that stereotype was true as he saw in front of him the monument of neglect and mediocrity. He was terribly tired and frustrated. There could not have been a deadlier combination than that for an angry Indian bureaucrat.

He worked in one of those departments in the government whose job is to churn out reports after reports, that everyone in the business of churning out reports knew, were useless. He worked in the department of Food and Public Distribution, a department whose job is to formulate policies on export and import of food and edible oils in India.

If one would have seen college photographs of Sitam it would have been difficult to imagine that someone with his looks, personality and erudition would work in a department such as this.

He used to, and in a lot of ways still looked stunning in his 5 feet 5 inches short Nepalese frame. Small eyes, bushy crop of hair, flat stomach and great skin – all gift of the genes that he in his own words 'had not lifted a grain to influence', for whom a bottle of Old Monk was a balm for the heart then and a source of meditation now. Although in his mind he should have become a swashbuckling police officer who broke bones and flew from high rises, and protected everyone from evil criminals, through a strange quirk of fate, he was now protecting large stocks of food grains from rodents and insects.

Sitam was in Mumbai on an errand for his senior officer and had absolutely no interest in being there. He was to stay in Hotel Landmark which only exacerbated his anger – of course he deserved better but then the miracles of Indian *babudom* are inexplicable not only to the common man but also to their own. His trip was for a full month and he had just arrived a week ago. Despite the deteriorating situation and increasing alarm, an earnest plea to his boss fell on deaf ears. He was asked to rise to the occasion and stay put in Mumbai – something he knew that his boss was forcing upon him for the utter lack of devotion that Sitam had so far demonstrated towards him. In general, such behaviour is bad but in the context of Indian bureaucracy, it's suicidal. It was only when he was buying his daily quota of Old Monk in the evening that he got to know about the 21-day lockdown. He would thank his survival skills much later but at that time it appeared only as a whim, he ordered a full crate of Old Monk from the Wine shop. He trudged into Hotel Landmark like a General victorious after war, struggling to carry the 12 bottles of Old Monk – a decision not only he, but also others will secretly thank him for over the next 21 days and more.

Manoj Joshi and his Mumbai team were on a frantic VC from a makeshift office in a shared building when they heard the news of the nationwide lockdown. It would still be an hour after the country came to know that he would come to know, because he was in an animated discussion with some financers on the other end of the video conferencing. His team knew it because their mobiles had started to buzz from concerned family members, however no one had the courage to take calls or visibly check their messages. All of this was done surreptitiously, for they knew if caught prying on their handsets by Manoj, would mean a consequence more draconian than the lockdown itself – or at least that was the reputation he carried.

In any case he was fighting a battle for survival of their company. They were acutely aware that if this funding did not come through, then there was going to be a long winter. Last few quarters had not been good for sales and some decisions by Manoj had not turned out to be the the winners they had been for many years. Many bankers had refused to extend the olive branch, and this was the last chance. Manoj was at his persuasive best and his elite educational background showed. He was lean, wore a crisp shirt and suit, and the rimless glasses only amplified his elegant look. He was a winner all the way. However, the circumstances they were in were not to his liking.

The questions from the other side were as disconcerting as were expected, although Manoj was impressive – deftly answering where it was required, carefully dodging where it was necessary, sharing facts and figures where it would buttress his argument and speaking in generalities where he had nothing worthwhile to show as evidence. MBAs have this ability in their toolkit. It's a survival guide for them – to be intelligent when needed and bullshit inanities when required; the latter more often than they cared to admit.

What his team did not know however, was that it was not only do or die for the company but also a do or die for Manoj. As a rising star quite used to winning, he knew that only through this deal could he wipe off the last few crappers and re-stablish his claim for the business head position – something that was due to open soon. A failure today meant that he could kiss goodbye his dream of becoming a business head before he turned thirty-five. This was personal to him.

It was during such a precariously perched point someone from the other side announced the lockdown and called for this meeting to be rescheduled. Manoj, fuming inside but maintaining a smile agreed pleasantly.

So when he walked into Hotel Landmark that evening he was infuriated on many counts – one on his company, who because of cost cutting had put him in this hotel, which was clearly not up to his tastes or standards; second, on the state of suspension of the outcome of this meeting and finally the realization that he was stuck in this godforsaken hotel for the next 21 days.

Razia Sheikh

While Sunil Paswan was watching the PM declaring the 21-day lockdown, and Kulwant Kaur was in a taxi on her way back to the hotel, Sitam Pradhan was buying a crate of Old Monk and Manoj Joshi was blissfully unaware of what was going on as he was in the flow of his presentation – Razia Sheikh was attending her husband's cousin's wedding. She had checked into this hotel much to the opposition of both her husband and the uncle's family but it was easier this way than to explain to all the nosey relatives why their nephew had not come but had sent his wife instead.

She needed some respite from those prying questions. This had been the state of affairs ever since their marriage. Her doctor husband was too busy treating patients and found attending such family gatherings a meaningless waste of time. He had happily outsourced the burden of fulfilling such family responsibilities to Razia, who would be part representative and part emissary in such gatherings. This was always a tricky situation, especially when your name is Razia Sheikh and your husband's name is Srijith Nair and you are representing him at a wedding from his side of the family. Hence, Hotel Landmark was a haven for Razia.

It had frustrated her to no extent that this wedding was even happening given the Corona scare, but it was not her remit. Her job was to attend. She saw the extended family, the gross display of gold and silk, the meaningless banter that accompanies such weddings and promised herself one more time that she would not attend them ever again. All wedding ceremonies bored her. Her own had bored her too.

If marriages were a redundant institution, then wedding ceremonies were the act formalising the act of perpetuating that redundancy – as if a ceremony would cause make a dead institution to somehow wake up.

She had somehow braved her own marriage. This did not mean that she did not love Srijith; both were head over heels in love with each other – they just did not feel the necessity for the elaborate functions that go with it. Her distaste for such crass display and irresponsible wastage of wealth was very thinly hidden. She walked into Hotel Landmark almost in relief from that ostentatiousness only to realise that she was stuck there for 21 days.

2. Gods can have feet of clay

Sitam

A night spent with Old Monk can have strange effects. I woke up with a very unusual thought on my mind. I realised after waking up thinking about waking up – how does one wake up really? What is the first emotion you feel as you wake up?

As the slumber wears off and you become aware of being alive, not yet having achieved complete awareness of your bearings, but only the awareness that you are indeed still there – what do you feel in those few uncorrupted seconds?

I smiled at my own question and allowed the thoughts to wander.

'Do I wake up with a feeling of some kind of heaviness?' There is no real reason to feel this way because everything is just fine, but the dawn of wakefulness is heavy, like the child who enters a dark room in his own house – he is comforted by the familiarity of the house and yet discomfited by the dark.

'Do I wake up with a feeling of a dull alarm that the body intuitively feels when it is in danger, uncorroborated by facts but is palpable in the bones, nevertheless?' There is no reason to feel this way for everything is fine but the dawn of wakefulness comes with an inexplicable anxiety, like moving in the jungle – comforted by our abilities to meander through it and yet acutely aware that you are in the wild.

'Do I wake up with a feeling of weightlessness, a feeling of no feeling at all?' I become aware of everything, my body, my surroundings, my situations and yet I feel nothing. I am here and yet I am not here. I levitate above and beyond, almost making fun of the mundane. I am untouched and detached. Actually, detached is not the right word – detachment is deliberate, a conscious attempt to severe attachment; this feeling is a stage deeper – as if I never had an anchor or ties. Like clouds.

'Do I wake up with a feeling of unadulterated joy?' – as if I feel like dancing the moment I become aware that I am awake. There is no reason to feel this way, but I am almost looking forward to getting up. There is a zing in my being that wants to give life a fresh shot. I almost surprise myself with this energy. It's like the mountain spring, which is hurtling down the slope, with no purpose but being purposive in the act of its flow.

'Do I wake up smiling?' I smile as the first shimmer of wakefulness emerges from the dark abyss of sleep. I have no reason to smile but I feel like smiling, there is some vague happiness that I know exists somewhere deep down, in the acute realisation that I have more than I need, in the comfort that I have more than what I thought I will ever have, in the thankfulness that I have more than what many others have. I wake up with gratitude although in this twilight of wakefulness and slumber I am not yet aware of the word 'gratitude'.

'Do I wake up in a hurry, an abruptness that is so jerky that it shatters the calm of the sleep and the joy of getting up?' As a kid, I had noticed an egg hatching and a cow giving birth to a calf in my village near Gangtok and was always intrigued about the slowness and the gradualness of the process. There was no abruptness to it. Abruptness kills. *Young children wake up gradually, adults wake up abruptly.*

I feel tired at my own chain of thoughts. I think this is what happens when you wake up in a hotel, hundreds of miles away from home, on the first day of what was an unprecedented lockdown in the life of a country.

As I got down for breakfast, I saw someone arguing with the manager at the front desk, whom I would later discover as someone who had a talent for arguing with everyone. He looked smart and articulate and as someone who was used to having his way. I heard the manager call him 'Manoj sir'.

I looked around the dining table and found two ladies at two different tables – one was old with a lot of silver in her hair and the other was 'South Indian types' – dusky, big eyes, clean skin, long thick black hair.

'How often we use these stereotypes to label people!' I thought to myself. I was amazed at the acceptability of judging someone like this and then my thoughts went back to how often I was called 'chinky' in my Delhi University days and how angry that would make me. I was doing the same thing right now and it did not occur to me as something wrong.

As I was wrapping up my breakfast the manager came in and got all of us together and introduced us all. He also described the situation that we were in because of the lockdown. He emphasised that we were only four of us in the hotel, that we were stuck here for the next 21 days, that we could not go out at all, that he would take utmost care of us during these 21 days, that he was working with a skeletal staff and hence service might not be as prompt as we thought, that he was moving us all to the same floor so that the rooms are close to each other, that we would meet downstairs for breakfast, lunch and dinner at 8.00 am, 1.00 pm and 8.00 pm sharp.

I think the enormity of the situation hit us only now. We were indeed stuck. We were four strangers in a strange city in a strange hotel stuck together for 21 days. It would turn out to be a lot longer than that, but we did not know it then.

We got together at the same table out of politeness or maybe out of the spirit of survival. This reminded me of our long-distance train travel during my childhood – the moment we would settle in, the first thing we would do was to know everyone around, ask questions around our destinations and other sundry things. We would share food, introduce each other, find as much common ground as possible, so that a sufficiently warm relationship would be forged for the duration of the journey. Many would convert into pen friends if not more. I realised how old I sounded. My son would not even know what a 'pen friend' was. I guess the same will happen here now. We would find some common ground between us all. .

We sat there for more than an hour introducing ourselves.

I liked Kulwant. She gave me the impression of someone who would comfort you merely by her presence. She said she was from Amritsar, husband was a businessman, and she had a son who had recently married and an unmarried daughter. I wondered why she was travelling alone.

Razia was a silent type. She hardly spoke. I am not

even sure if she was listening to whatever inanities we were talking about. She was there and yet not there. However, she looked pretty much at ease with herself. Not sure if she was even worried.

I hated Manoj already. Maybe I started to hate him when I saw him arguing with the manager earlier. He reminded me of all those hostel seniors in my DU days who treated me as shit while ragging me as a fresher – full of entitlement, bossy, and giving this vibe that intelligence and position made them superior to everyone else, as if the world owed them reverence and an immediate servility. I remind myself to hate Manoj even when I do not have a reason to.

We disperse to our rooms with an agreement to meet at 1.00 pm for lunch.

Kulwant

I am not even sure what I am doing here. This is not how it was supposed to turn out. I can't share my turmoil at home because that will infuriate them even more. They were against this trip from the moment I shared the idea with them. How do I tell everyone at home – husband, son and daughter that I would have gone mad had I not done this; however crazy they might think I am.

Sixty-two years and it appears that I have not lived a day for myself. I was born in a village in the district Gurdaspur, not far from the border, although the family originally belonged to Lyallpur, which now is called Faisalabad. During the British Raj, the city Lyallpur was named in honour of the then Lieutenant-Governor of Punjab, Sir James Broadwood Lyall, for his services in the colonisation of the lower Chenab

Valley. In 1979, the Government of Pakistan changed the name of the city from Lyallpur to Faisalabad, in honour of King Faisal of Saudi Arabia, who made several financial contributions to Pakistan.

I remember all the furore that happened recently on naming and renaming of roads and cities – I think this shit has been going on for for longer than we care to remember. I remember asking my father what Lyallpur was called before it was called Lyallpur. He thought my question was stupid, which basically meant he did not know the answer. I had learnt over the years that when an adult calls a child's question stupid, it often means that he doesn't know the answer.

I remember the furore it created when I fell in love with a Muslim boy– it was a scandal for its time. The society around me was shocked as if I had betrayed the country and my father was shocked because he felt I had betrayed all the pain he and his family had to bear during partition, as if I had betrayed everything they held dear and lost in Lyallpur.

I learnt so many things in those days as this news broke. I realised that human beings are more worried about protecting memories, particularly of grief than about protecting happiness and joy in the future. They do not want to betray the past – as if becoming happy now would mean you have betrayed the pain of the past. The only way to keep respecting that pain was to remain chained to it. One could not flirt with happiness or liberation because it would mean you have forgotten the anguish of the past – and that is sacrilege. The past had to be remembered daily.

Only the death of parents liberates the child from the chains of the parents' past. This can neither be hastened nor wished.

I was able to stand against my parent's opposition somehow but the boy I loved could not. He backed out after a while, unable to deal with the repeated emotional onslaught from his family, the details of which appear hazy now and irrelevant too. I have never forgiven him – not for backing out of course, which I had soon realised was the least of my problems. In hindsight I am not confident how that relationship would have turned out, maybe very good or maybe it would have crumbled under its own contradictions. Predicting the success of marriages is pure betting – 'jua'.

The real damage of that fiasco was that I stopped standing for what I wanted thereafter. I was no longer sure if what I wanted was even worth it. I married, had children, raised them and took care of my husband's family with all the sincerity I had. I was happy in every which way we are taught to be happy – had more than sufficient to eat, wear and enjoy. However, there was this small hole that gnawed at my soul all the time – will I be able to wish for something purely for myself? Can I ask any more with confidence? Can I desire something without hesitation? It was this that I had been struggling with for many years now and it was this that made me take the decision that brought me here to this hotel.

I convinced my family that I want to visit the holy gurudwaras of Bidar in Karnataka and Nanded in Maharashtra, where the last of our Gurus, Guru Gobind Singh breathed his last. I would also like to visit the birthplace of Saint Namdev near Pandharpur, also in Maharashtra. Namdev, who was Maharashtrian by birth has a strong following in parts of Punjab – in fact he died there. Everyone knew my interest in spirituality and the bhakti saints, so they accepted my idea of a solo trip – what to them was pilgrimage for religion, was to me a pilgrimage for liberation.

Everyone had their lunch in solitude. It was during dinner time some conversation started to flow.

'The PM has a penchant for such radical and mostly poorly thought out grand plans,' said Sitam while munching his rotis.

'You must be a Congress supporter,' pat came the jibe by Manoj.

'Excuse me?' asked Sitam. 'How did you arrive at that great conclusion?'

'You guys only find a reason to criticise the PM – he is the best option we have. See how much respect he has brought to the country internationally. He is strong willed and even Pakistan fears him now,' said Manoj.

'But I thought we were discussing the COVID lockdown and its preparation!' Sitam muttered as he chewed.

'So, you think someone could have done a better job – who is as good as him? Look around and tell me who could have handled this better than him?' Manoj sounded impatient.

'But no one else is the PM of the country – I can only opine on what he is doing or not doing or should be doing,' said Sitam, with a certain edge to his voice.

'It's people like you who constantly criticise him despite knowing no one is as hard working as he – do you know he sleeps for less than 4 hours and the rest of the time he is working for us?' added Manoj.

'Of course – he has a job and he is doing it to the best of his ability – at least I hope so,' replied Sitam.

'Is there anything that you don't like in him – I mean you seem to be a diehard supporter of him; in your eyes is there anything at all that you believe he could improve or do better or you wish he changed in himself or in the manner he did things?'

This was a curved ball from Sitam. Everyone else was quiet but enjoying the show. One could see a slight hesitation in Manoj's voice, which he tried to camouflage in the name of taking a large bite. He was buying time to frame the argument.

The hiatus in the conversation allowed sufficient time for Razia to pitch in. 'Even Gods can have feet of clay.'

'What do you mean?' asked an irritated Manoj.

'Here is my point – the moment a large group of people put all their hopes on one person and start to believe, if not fantasise, that he is the messiah who will pull them out of their current rot; that if not for this person we are doomed because no one else has either the vision or the ability or the charisma to lead us through – these people are creating conditions for either disappointment or failure or both.'

'So, are you saying that there is a problem in acknowledging that he is the best that we have because he is not perfect?' Asked Manoj – 'Remember others are even worse!'

'I am not saying that. All I am saying is that the belief that ONE person, worse still ONE specific person will miraculously change things for the better – be able to provide direction to the lost, provide vision to the blind, energise the sleepy, spark up the mediocre and wave the magic wand – and voila everything will be hunky dory, then I suspect we are creating conditions for either disappointment or failure,' argued Razia.

So far, no one had imagined that Razia could be so forceful or deep. Manoj had not imagined this rebuttal to come from her – Sitam yes, but Razia no.

Razia continued – 'Such hero worship, romantic as the idea may sound, is flawed in multiple ways and often ends in grief.'

'One – such an obsessive cult often distorts vision. The idea of a messiah or a miracle man is fiction. It sounds great in myths and stories, but real people have real abilities. They come with their expertise but also with their handicaps. Such expectations make the journey of improvement led by one person either too simplistic or worse, delusional. This phenomenon takes eyes away from the complexity of reality and puts disproportionate focus on the personality. It takes away attention from daily dirty work required to be accomplished by many more and focuses on the futile ritual of hero worship.'

'Second – while it is great for the leader who is at the receiving end of such adulation, it is damaging to the masses – the very people who are waiting for this messiah. In the act of depending way too much on one person, the masses relinquish their free will, often without being aware of it. They abdicate their own role in the process of progress, almost saying "since I cannot do, let me be unquestionably loyal to someone who I THINK can." Loyalty is not a substitute for the spirit of ownership – it leads to a voluntary disempowerment.'

'Third – this creates fertile ground for such a messiah to become a tyrant. One only needs to study history to know that every single dictator began his journey as the ONLY hope to his people. Benevolent dictator is either a myth or a precursor to an absolute dictator. Megalomaniacs and overblown egos draw their sustenance from flattering masses and adulating employees. The system is voluntarily handing over the power of collective and concentrating it in one individual – all in the name of support.'

'Fourth – Any leader in any context when burdened with unrealistic expectations of magic – that only he will solve all problems, create prosperity and growth, only he will arrest depleting profitability and bring back glory and the rest, is quite likely to disappoint. It is not a question of the person's ability, but the odds get stacked against him with such a huge burden of expectations. The absoluteness of the hope from him will make even a slip look like a fall.'

There was stunned silence at the table. Razia was the only one with an amazing calm on her face. She did not feel exerted with the long monologue. It was as if she had practiced it so many times. It was as if this was not the first time she was talking about this.

Manoj was visibly shaken. 'So, what do you suggest we should do – start criticising the only hope that we have, start to poke holes in everything he does, demean and discourage his steps – as your ilk seem to do?'

Razia fired her final salvo – 'No I am not suggesting that. All I am suggesting is do believe in Gods but remember, even Gods can have feet of clay.'

3. Roti, Kapda *aur* Network

'*Kaise hain Paswan ji?*' asked Kulwant as she passed him on the counter.

'*Pagalpan hai madam,*' answered Sunil Paswan.

'The world is coming to an end. There is madness all around during this lockdown. Our regular supplier boys were beaten by the police during delivery. We have not got our regular supplies for today even after the announcements were made that they would not be stopped. Half of my boys have called back to say they are too afraid to come to work.'

'Hope we have enough for us,' asked Kulwant.

'Don't you worry madam – there is enough for all of you; after all there are only four of you,' answered Sunil.

'Five – including you,' smiled Kulwant and walked towards the breakfast area to find Razia eating alone in a corner.

'You were in a fiery mood yesterday' began Kulwant.

Razia smiled sheepishly. 'I think I went overboard. I don't know what came over me.'

'But you did make a lot of sense. I have felt the same about messiahs all my life. It's just that they are not political leaders in my case. Every grown up in a family behaves like a messiah for the young ones – as if they control our lives and destinies. Children also believe that the elders are too big, too strong, too good, too mature and too sensible. Only as they grow up, they realise all of that is not really true. Parents and elders are all like us – fragile, wrong, insecure, weak, and most of the times not worthy of our blind reverence,' said Kulwant.

It was Razia's turn to be surprised at the depth and significance of what Kulwant had spoken. 'Every strand of grey hair has a story,' thought Razia to herself.

Since Kulwant kept quiet after that she almost felt disappointed because it was clear Kulwant was only beginning. She had more to speak, more to bare, more to unload. Since she became quiet suddenly, it felt much quieter than how quiet appears.

'The unsaid is also an amazing thing,' – said Razia to herself. 'It has a charm to it.'

'You need to keep reminding yourself of the obvious; charm lies in the unsaid, the unwritten, and the un-displayed. It takes mastery to control silence,' she remembered reading somewhere.

Youth is usually verbose and expressive, fuelled by the exuberance that usually comes with naivety, idealism or foolhardiness. Middle-age is the wearing out of them all. Most lives are a struggle to overcome the threat of that ordinariness. In that sense, most lives are a struggle not with their circumstances but with themselves. What can be scarier than ordinariness staring back from the mirror. It takes quite a lot to come to terms with the fact that having reached a certain age one is at best still a work-in-progress.

One must speak on anything and quite liberally, for in our ability to speak with abandon, lies our sense of liberation. It's like the adolescent who has the freedom to go anywhere and who because he has that freedom, shall exercise it without restraint. The fun is not in the freedom per se but in the realization that the freedom can be exercised at will. It is only with time that one realizes that the 'charm lies in the unsaid, the unwritten and the un-displayed'.

What is already expressed and articulated, in speech or words, is like cards that are already revealed. They do not hold much power or promise. The spoken and articulated do not hold potential for modification and correction. Finally, they also do not hold any more charm – for charm lies in the unexplored. What is already explored is largely boring. Unknown holds the power of imagination and excitement.

What is it that makes speaking irresistible? Why is it that having the last word in a in the conversation is such an aphrodisiac? There is grace in the quiet. There is mystery in silence. There is power in the unsaid. Razia had experienced that power just now in the unsaid of Kulwant.

Razia

This trip is turning out to be a roller coaster ride. Nothing about my life in any case is without drama. The more I run away from drama, the more drama enters my life. How much I envy those who can live peacefully.

I was only 21 when I got married to Srijith in Kozhikode. Srijith was an idealist, with dreams in his eyes about changing the world. He had become a doctor only recently and contrary to his batch mates he wanted to be a doctor in a government hospital and serve in the small villages. I think his idealism came from his story. His father died in the 1982 hooch tragedy when he was only a young boy. The family shifted to Kozhikode thereafter and they somehow scrapped through the twin challenge of survival and education. It was his great desire to serve that pulled him through all those years. I was young and naive, and it was not difficult to be pulled towards him and his idealism.

Naivety is a prerequisite for idealism. The well informed and mature can rarely afford idealism.

My marriage to Srijith was not without its own drama. Oh no – not the classical Hindu-Muslim drama but the other drama of rich and poor. Relatively speaking, I was more affluent; my family was well educated and of course he was the proverbial poor boy but more damagingly, resolute in his ambition to remain poor. Nothing can be more damaging to the prospects of Indian marriages, particularly the love mutant of it, than a groom whose life's ambition is to serve the needy. A bride's father can deal with infirmities and difference of religion, but the prospect of lifelong penury can deter even the most broad-minded parents. Back in those days when I announced my decision to marry Srijith, it was his idealism that was the greatest barrier.

Srijith continues to work for the downtrodden. Unfortunately, God is giving him many opportunities in the recent years – during the recent Kerala floods or the deadly Nipah virus outbreak.

We have been married for a decade and I happily remain in the shadows. People ask me if someone as educated as me should waste my life doing nothing. It is difficult for me to explain my mind to them. Everyone does not derive meaning from money or success or power. I derive meaning from doing what I like, which at different points of time is different things. The money that Srijith brings is more than enough and I do not feel in any way incomplete or insufficient or undervalued because I do not earn money. Maybe it's because Srijith does not make me feel so or maybe I would have felt this way irrespective – I don't know.

I have very limited needs and hence the lure of power or money has had limited sway over me. Maybe one day I will regret this passivity or maybe not. I will decide when such a thing happens.

I like to look outside the window for hours. Watching the sky uplifts me. I listen to the noise of the winds. I enjoy the sun shining on my face. I love reading. I love the quiet. I love not talking to anyone. I love just lying down, what others call slowing down, is my natural speed.

Many ask me what would have happened if this love story with Srijith would not have materialised. Since I was the one who had proposed to Srijith, what would have happened if Srijith had not responded positively?

I wonder what it is about unrequited love that makes it the fancy of all human beings? Cinema, poetry, prose and in some ways all form of fine arts would have been deprived of so much inspiration had love found its fulfilment. Statistically speaking, love finding its reciprocation is an exception, if not an aberration. Yet an entire cottage industry of expression and literature not only draws inspiration but actually draws sustenance from its failure to be reciprocated.

Some would argue that precisely because of this that love has this widespread appeal – providing fertility to the painter's imagination or converting an ordinary individual into a potential poet. There would be no romanticism left in life if love were to be reciprocated. How deserted and arid, how hopeless and uninspiring life would be without the elixir of what-if's!

The more I witness the canvass of artists, the span of cinema, the depths of poetry and the expanse of prose, the more I am convinced that the story of human sensibilities is shaped by the stories of love and its various variants of un-fulfilment.

It would also be a folly to believe that there ever existed a thing called absolute fulfilment in the matters of the heart. Each story around us is only a work in progress at best and completely unrequited at worst. The first provides struggle, the second much needed angst.

Some love stories are stories of bereavement, others are stories of anger, yet others are stories of tragedy; some are stories of exhaustion, others are stories of errors, and the most tragic of all are the stories which are about the IDEA of love.

So, what is it that makes it so much talked about, so much written about, so much mused about – this whole thing about love attaining some kind of permanence? Well I guess, precisely this pursuit of an impossible utopia makes it so popular in everyone's imagination. Everyone knows the utopia does not exist, but its pursuit is so seductively idealistic. The idea of love is so pure in its construct, that there is inspiration even in the failure to find it.

Unrequited love seems to be a cottage industry, and everyone is milking it. I milked it too. I guess Srijith got milked in the process.

Sunil Paswan came to meet everyone during dinner that day and excitedly showed the images and news that he was receiving on his WhatsApp from across the country.

He showed there was a Baba somewhere who was talking about how drinking cow urine and applying cow dung would prevent the spread of Corona. He also showed how the policemen were controlling the creatively inclined who had taken the lockdown with insufficient seriousness. There were news and short videos about how police made liberal use of their lathis to deal with such liberties in some places and how they asked people to squat and hold their ears in other places – a type of punishment that reminded them of their school days. He was particularly amused when he shared the case where police made the strollers jump like jump like frogs.

There is something about humour that is so linked to class. Different things tickle people of different classes. The sense of humour evolves with education and then one looks down on the sense of humour of the ones lower down the pecking order.

For Sunil Paswan all that he was rattling from his WhatsApp forwards was comical. All the TikTok videos around husbands and wives were infinitely funny to him. The more slapstick the humour the more acute was the relief. Yet to others not only did it not appear funny, it also appeared tacky and offensive.

Sunil had climbed up the social ladder steadily since the time he landed in Mumbai, from doing odd jobs, to becoming a doorman, to the front office boy to finally becoming the manager. In his mind he had acquired the knowhow of dealing with customers, managing books of accounts, operating the computer and talking with confidence with those who were more educated than him, little knowing that this journey of progress would hit a roadblock while ascertaining what he considered as humorous and what the thoroughbred considered as funny.

'Is there anything else you all would need to make your stay comfortable?' he asked everyone in general and no one in particular.

Razia shook her head lazily meaning there was nothing that she needed.

Sitam asked him for a bucket of ice to be sent to his room and gave everyone a smile and asked, 'Anyone wants to join?'

Kulwant asked if she could get some jaggery after food – this was her post-dinner routine back in Amritsar.

Manoj asked, 'Can the network be improved?'

'What?' asked Sunil not quite comprehending the request.

'Can the Wi-Fi be improved – the signals are poor,' explained Manoj. Manoj added with a smile. 'Wi-fi comes before Wi-fe; I would be morose without the latter, but I shall be poor without the former.' He attempted his hand at tacky humour, which clearly did not go down quite well.

'Roti, Kapda *aur* Network,' are the three basic needs, quipped Manoj.

4. Guilt is a Manufactured Emotion

Manoj

I have always hated the mediocre. I have hated those who peddle mediocrity as a virtue even more. I do not suffer the average easily. I like people who get things done. I like those who take charge, who fight for what they stand for and what they desire. I appreciate those who will not take no for an answer, even when what they are asking for, is unreasonable – for only such people create magic. In any case who decides what is reasonable?

I do not want the weak, the meek and those who themselves are incapable of getting things done to decide what qualifies as reasonable.

I have little patience for those who are nice for the sake of being nice. I don't want such people around me or in my team or my social circle. I find meekness loathsome, and their attempt to rub that meekness on me repulsive. They camouflage their weaknesses as an essential quality of human beings and expect patience from me – and that I have not an ounce of!

I like the go-getters – the ones who will not sit or tire till the job is done irrespective of the methods or the price. Good is grossly overplayed. They must know that there are reasons and there are results and the former do not matter.

The world has moved forward on the shoulders of those who refused to accept excuses and reasons and thank God for that! Corporations have been built, technology, science, discoveries and inventions have been achieved by the bull-headed, the thick-skinned, the unreasonable. I also believe they have not got their due – the world enjoys the fruits of their doggedness but hates their style.

I like to win – actually, I am a sore loser. I have always been like that, ever since I was a young boy. I had to compete to get everything that I have today. I had to be relentless to get toys as a young kid, fight with my elder brother to get a space in the common room we shared in the 2 BHK we lived in, had to slog my ass off to be noticed in school because I would always be the 'younger brother of Nikhil', who incidentally was a remarkable student and athlete. I loved him then and I love him now and I am glad that I had him in my life. I could have never had a better benchmark to compare with; it is a different matter that over time my own achievements were no less than his.

My parents loved him and me both although he had the advantage of being the first one. One thing was very clear, I was destined to always play the second inning – he always had the upper hand of getting to set the standards. In a lot of ways, even if I bettered his record in studies or sports or achievements, it was never good enough because my own achievements were always recorded in terms of 'vis-à-vis Nikhil'. Sometimes I wonder what a profound thing it is to be born second.

Coming back to my story, my father was a government servant and so hard work and education were the only ways we could overcome our circumstances. He was a person with a very strong sense of right and wrong, which I think both of us imbibed. We grew up in Nagpur and then I did my MBA from Ahmedabad in 2001-2003. We were largely apolitical as a family, but I have watched politics very closely, first in Nagpur and then Ahmedabad.

I have always worked hard ever since I was a young kid. Winning and being good enough was never a question. Soon winning became second nature to me. I have benefited immensely from this frame of looking at things – I always scored great, went to great colleges, got great jobs and grew up very fast in my organisation. I get things done and I make things happen and as I said I have little patience for the rest.

My friends have believed that I am argumentative, but I believe I have better arguments. It's just that they try to camouflage the weakness of their arguments and the flaccidity of their spirit by describing me as bad. In a world full of mediocrity, excellence can often be mistaken as arrogance. I have been called arrogant for so long now that it no longer matters. In the earlier days it used to hurt a bit because I felt misunderstood but now it feels like a validation of my abilities. I have never seen someone better than me calling me arrogant – why is it that only those who cannot win label me as rude and arrogant?

I believe power is important. It is a tool to get things done. It's a vehicle. Yes, I know that absolute power corrupts absolutely and all that shit – and that is why I have never liked Spiderman movies. Maybe I like Thanos – and while children can be forgiven for seeing him as a villain, I am shocked that well-meaning and educated adults also see him as a villain; no one sees that his power is for progress and betterment.

Do not get me wrong – I am not propagating dictatorship or absolutism; I am only saying that sometimes you need the decisive to do the right things and you don't always have the luxury of consensus and time for asking everyone for their views. Revolutions do not happen by taking approvals – they must just be done.

I have always admired strong leaders. I take great inspiration from their grit and their doggedness. I like stories about their resoluteness amidst small obstacles and large. I have a very simple principle about leadership – 'get it done'.

I don't remember feeling guilty much of my life. This does not mean that I have nothing that in normal circumstances for normal people would evoke guilt.

However, guilt, like many other things as beauty, love, revenge and spite, lies in the bosom of the beholder – and so when it came to the choice of feeling guilty for a misdemeanour, I have usually chosen the better path of brushing it aside as an essential part of coming-of-age ritual, a small price for progress.

Amongst the many human emotions which are of the same family as guilt, such as possessiveness, grief, jealousy, and anger, I would rate guilt as the deadliest. It is like diabetes – not really a disease, but a disorder that kills you slowly but definitively. It is almost as if guilt enjoys the process of killing you.

It only becomes worse with time. Like diabetes, it does not kill by itself, but actually creates a shutdown in all other organs, particularly the heart. Having a heart in itself Maybe bad but a guilt-ridden heart is much worse.

Guilt normally begins like a small cut and then it feeds on itself and it grows and grows. Soon you are engulfed in its octopus like grip, questioning your own worth and goodness. Guilt is an auto-immune disaster – you start feeding on yourself.

In fact, I believe that 'guilt' is an established business around us these days. Guilt is a manufactured emotion!

We must realise one essential thing about guilt – it is an emotion that is literally taught to be felt. Sadness, depression, grief, disappointment, hurt and other emotions happen automatically to us. No one really teaches us how and in what circumstances it must be experienced. We just respond with them according to circumstances.

Guilt is hideously different. A tiger feels no guilt in killing the deer – but we are taught early on that killing needs repentance because it is wrong.

Guilt is an organised crime against free-willed souls.

This is how the whole thing works. One designs an elaborate code which teaches us all the places where if one is not pandering to the established norms, one is supposed to feel bad about it. The keyword is 'supposed to' – meaning that someone else is governing for us what we must be feeling bad about. The greater the experienced misery, the better is the atonement! The guilt must not only be felt, but it must also be visibly expressed; there is nothing called guilt in private! The whole drama about guilt is staged around an explicit performance of atonement.

Finally, the funny thing about guilt is this – if for some strange reason you have discovered that this business of guilt is something that is a cart load of crap and you don't really feel like feeling guilty, then the guardians of guilt will make you feel guilty about not feeling guilty – *'see how shameless you are – not even feeling guilty'*, they would often say. It is big business if not an outright scam.

Sunil Paswan was the newsreader in the hotel. It was becoming customary for everyone to check with him the latest news. While they would ask the question out of social politeness, Paswan would dutifully rattle out the headlines.

'The government has announced a strong economic package for the poor and all to deal with the lockdown, to the tune of almost 1.70 lakhs crores – only time will tell whether it is good enough or not.'

'21 dead in India, the numbers tested positive more than 800 – it's becoming bigger by the day sirjee' announced a grim looking Sunil Paswan.

'But I am very happy to know that America has become the country with the highest numbers of infected — numbers crossing half a million,' chuckled the news reporter from Hotel Landmark.

'There is news of police using their lathis liberally across the country – we are funny people sir – we like to stay at home when we are allowed to go out, and we like to go out when we are stopped,' this time it was the philosopher Mr. Paswan.

'Do you know this coronavirus is conspiracy of China, sirjee – to wreak havoc across the world so that it can become the most powerful country in the world?' – He asked that day to the guests of Hotel Landmark at the dinner table when he came to check if everything was okay. He asked that question and left. The question never left the table though.

'You think this is a conspiracy?' Manoj asked no one in particular.

Sitam considered it as a question directed to him and took it upon himself to answer.

'Quite possible – they have been trying to become the next superpower for a long time now. They have the money; they have the numbers and most importantly they have the resolve. There is nothing more purposive than a hunger to dominate, to rule, to be the most powerful.'

'It also leads to dreadful consequences,' came a calm voice. This was Kulwant.

'What do you mean?' asked Manoj

'Don't you know everything that happened every time there was a set of people who believed they are more powerful than others, or that the world owed them more than what they had? – This wanting more has created demons,' said Kulwant, calm and composed.

Even Manoj did not respond – not because he could not counter the argument but because there was something deeply painful in the manner in which Kulwant was speaking.

'Last year around the same time, I had a chance to visit the holocaust museum in the USA while I was there to attend a wedding – and do you know what was written outside its walls? – "The next time you witness hatred, the next time you see injustice, the next time you see genocide, THINK ABOUT WHAT YOU SAW TODAY."

'Have you ever met someone who has been a part of the partition?' she asked and looked around. Not one nodded.

'The partition of India, at both its borders – the western side and the eastern side, was equally inhuman and complex. For all of you it's a chapter you have read in some book but for many that grief is embedded in their bones. You are indifferent to it because it happened to others — even though you might be compassionate about it, you cannot really relate to it.

'You might say that you have some idea of pain – of some other kind. You may say that you identify with the pain because you can generally identify with any pain as you have an evolved sense of empathy. However, all pain is different. It hurts differently. Grief *is infinitely personal.*

'The upheaval, the distortion, the scars, the anger, the anguish is personal. It is felt through the stories told, the albums revisited, the diaries read and re-read. It is felt through the loss of family fortune – either to be permanently lost or through its redemption thereafter. The generations succeeding them have no choice but to stay invested in these stories. They will never know how, but they will own the partition and its echoes in strange ways – as if it is a family heirloom, passed from one generation to the next. *Pain is a funny inheritance. You cannot wish it away.'*

There was a deep silence at the table. No one wanted to be the culprit who shattered that silence through the sledgehammer of words.

It was Razia who did that. Thank God it was Razia. Her words were not the blow of a sledgehammer – they were the caress of a butterfly.

'Are you disturbed by all the evil that you see in the world?' she asked Kulwant.

'The world is not good or bad. The world just is – my father used to say this,' murmured Kulwant.

'All of us have a story. Every life had, has and will have stories. The play of events change, the characters swap places and the vile tide of time plays out the torment in different ways. There is nothing original in this – it seems all that has happened will only repeat itself – like war, separation, love, death, penury and hurt – only the theatre changes. However, what it elicits in each one of us is absolutely original – each one has her own cross to carry and it does seem heavier than the cross others are carrying.'

'Have you ever found a soul unsullied by his tumult?'

'All of us have a view about the inherent nature of things – often as unforgiving and cruel, depressing and dark, heavy and foreboding. Once that is done then conclusion precedes experience – even before things unravel, the sense of injustice, betrayal and disappointment is established. The world is certified as bad. This then becomes the default opinion for all future interactions and experiences. Life no longer is given a chance to prove otherwise.

'The world is. It is not good or bad. It just *is*!

'The world has no duties towards me – of being fair and nice, of being good and kind, of doing to me what I want and giving me what I desire! The world does not owe me anything in return for my efforts, loyalties and emotions – it does not have to take care of me. The world just *is*!' finally ended Kulwant.

'That makes a lot of sense Kulwant,' said Razia. 'It

offers me hope, frees me from the grasp that circumstances and events have over my ability to be happy. In the act of recognising the world as just something to be dealt with clinically, without the encumbrance of emotion and expectation, I free myself from that yoke of disappointment – that cancer that eats away life slowly but surely.'

Just then the phone rang – it was Sitam's. He picked up his phone and stepped out. Sitam returned in about half an hour and it was clear that everything was not all right. The furrows of worry were clear on his head and the usually confident Sitam Pradhan was visibly shaken.

'My son in Bangalore lives in a PG and the landlord has asked him to vacate the room immediately as he is closing the PG because of the Corona scare,' announced Sitam – 'and he has nowhere to go at this hour.'

There is nothing more heart wrenching than to see a helpless parent.

The next hour or so went in frantic calls by everyone. Everyone called someone who could help out the young boy in Bangalore. Finally, it was Razia who came to the rescue; she had an uncle who lived somewhere close to the PG of the boy's. Strings were pulled and the uncle took the boy to his home and it was agreed that he will stay there until an alternative arrangement is made.

If evil can surprise us, human kindness possesses no less an ability to surprise. It is uplifting to know that someone who till a moment ago meant nothing to you was willing to go through trouble for your sake. One has to go through this moment to know how it feels! Those who are deprived of this experience have missed out on such a beautiful aspect of life – they often die with a heart unfamiliar with kindness and in a way, it can be said of them, that they have never lived.

5. What is your Burden?

'What is it to be secure?' asked the little sparrow to her mother as she clung to her bosom.

They were in a nest, warm with twigs and branches. The nest had been made painstakingly over a long stretch of time – one twig and leaf at a time. It was a labour of love by the mother sparrow. The nest was hoisted upon two strong branches of a very large tree. The tree was the biggest in that area and everyone wanted their nest only on that tree for the strength it provided.

All birds vied, and some fought for a space on the branches of this big tree. It was not uncommon to see even sparrows fighting for space on this tree – sparrows that were known to be delicate and friendly otherwise. Aggression in eagles and vultures is nature but sparrows fighting is an acquired behaviour. Life in a jungle can make for strange sights. The search for security can bring out the worst even in sparrows.

So, the mother sparrow was very proud of herself that she had built this nest on this tree. The memory of how it was built might be hazy, but her pride was fresh. Her sense of security was fresh and intact. She flew all around the jungle, secure in the comfort that she could return to this warm nest on the strongest tree. She flew with confidence, mingled with other sparrows, went about her life with this sense of security. The nest gave her security. The tree gave her security.

The mother sparrow thought about all of this as she pondered over the question of the little sparrow. There was something about the question that she could not shrug off.

Life in the jungle continued unabated. The mornings and the nights fell just as they had for a million years. Seasons came and went and even though every day seemed like a new one, she often wondered if they were really new. Sparrows have been doing this for hundreds of years now – the getting up in the morning with the warm morning sun filtering through the leaves, the flying all around searching for worms and returning to their nests as the night fell.

This sparrow might believe her journey is unique and her struggle for survival is unique – but uniqueness is such an overrated pursuit. It is important to search for it, for otherwise life in the jungle could become so boring. The idea that all of this has happened a million times before and no one ever got out of it alive can be depressing. So, they weave a narrative that the jungle will last forever, and the nest will keep them warm and secure forever. The mother sparrow brushed these thoughts aside as she talked to the little one about how secure this nest was on this big strong tree. She wondered if she was telling this story to her little one or to herself.

It was almost without warning that the storm came. The winds were ferocious, and the rains were lethal, and the lightning was fatal. It was the first time the little one was seeing all of this. She clung to the mother even more tightly searching for security. The jungle had seen nature's fury before also, and so had the mother sparrow but for the little one, it was the first time. The wind was making the strong tree sway perilously. She was surprised and shocked for she always believed the tree to be strong. She could not imagine that even this tree could be made to sway and bring it so close to being uprooted. Her shock was on the border of disillusionment. The warm nest was slowly filling with water and with that the warmth that it always provided went away. There was a real chance that they would drown in the very nest that was home and had provided them security all this while. The twigs were untangling by the moment and suddenly the nest was no longer warm or secure. It was just a matter of time before they had to take the decision to abandon the nest and the tree. The young sparrow looked into the eyes of the mother sparrow with so many questions, and for the first time she realised that the mother sparrow did not have answers or was unsure of what to do.

The moment that was hanging over their head soon arrived. The young sparrow and the mother sparrow fluttered their wings and hesitantly flew out of the nest they had called home for so long. They struggled to keep themselves flying through the storm and flew out to a safe place amidst some rocks nearby.

It was clear to the little one that it was the strength in their wings that gave them security – neither the nest, nor the strength or size of the tree.

Sitam woke up from this dream feeling drained. The lines between life and dreams can be fuzzy sometimes. He thought of the events of last evening. He had kept on thinking late into the night about the fragility of parenting. We worry, fret and overthink to keep our children safe and secure without knowing what it even means to keep them secure. Is it even possible to keep them safe and secure from all things vile and dangerous and is it even a good thing? Would his son look at his experience of last evening for the rest of his life as something that he was glad he went through?

He thanked the sparrow in his dreams.

Sitam

I don't even remember the last time I felt I belonged somewhere. Trust me, only those who have lived the lives of being strangers in their circumstances can know what I have felt all my life.

I grew up in a little village about 10 kms from Gangtok where my father was a small businessman. Growing up in the mountains is an education in itself. More people learn about life in the shadows of the mountains and travelling through them instead of schools.

There are many ways in which just playing in the mountains and the vagaries it entails makes you learn vital life lessons.

There was this one time when I ventured on to a slope only a few kilometres from my home. Children did not follow routines then the way they follow these days in the cities – sometimes I feel sorry for my son that he does not even know what he is missing, as he has no experience of growing up without a schedule and not caring a fig about time. Then I realise it was only me who had instilled – or at least tried to. *There is no greater burden for a child than the unfulfilled lives of his parents.*

So, I remember this time when I started to walk up the mountain near my village. I stared at the mountains partly in awe and partly in fear. They stood there imposing their presence on everyone who dared to look at them, not caring for the emperor or the pauper – for they were drunk with the arrogance of their steep slopes. The mountains knew that being the emperor or the pauper made no difference to the climb. The difference amongst the status of the climbers was pertinent only to the world out there.

I had always wanted to be a king – most powerful, rich and prosperous and most importantly powerful. As I grew up I had looked at all the kings and queens of kingdoms, small and large, shown on TV and the books I read and experienced a tinge of envy. I had wanted to wear their robes, their crowns, and their regalia and be treated with similar sense of veneration by one and all. As I stared at the mountains, I was amused at that naivety of all those years – for it dawned upon me that in front of these mountains the difference between the courtier and the emperor was meaningless, almost laughable.

As I started to walk the partially visible trail up, left behind by the climbers before me I realized that I could not rely on the trail alone. Grass had grown around the trail and rocks had fallen over time, making the old trail partially invisible and unreliable. I realized I had to create my own trail.

Mountain slopes can be very treacherous. The slopes change. They change their contours and curves. Old footholds become slippery and new footholds emerge, if only one has the keen eye to find them and the courage to test them for firmness and grip.

I had to remind myself constantly that this climb was my climb and not someone else's. The trails would also have to be mine.

As I kept moving, the sun kept playing hide and seek with the clouds. In the mountains the sun appears more flirtatious than it does so in the plains. The sun could also be hard on the skin even as the air would be chilly. One could not depend on the sun at all times for its benevolent presence. I would have to climb even when it was dark, comforted by the realisation that the sun would be back any moment. In those moments of darkness, the best thing would have been to stay put, rest a while and not try too hard. Waiting patiently is an important part of the climb. I wondered if I was thinking too much instead of just putting one step forward.

When seen from a distance the peaks were visible constantly to me; I could set my eyes on them and move in that direction. However, I realized as I moved up, the peak, the destination would often move out of my sight. It would peep out only once in a while as a reminder of why I was here. Mostly it was only the next curve, the next ledge, the next boulder that had to be crossed. *In a lot of ways, the top was irrelevant. The next boulder was.*

I was not unaccustomed to climbing mountains. I had done it before. I could feel my excitement returning from the previous climb, but I could also feel my fears returning. I remembered a conversation with a villager once – *this mountain was notorious for rockslides.*

Every mountain has its own tantrums. Some known for steepness, some for slipperiness, and some for no trails – this one was known for rockslides. The villager had told me to be cautious. Look for tell-tale signs of an impending rockslide. He had asked me to keep looking for loose rocks and falling pieces however small. If the small ones are there, the big ones would come soon after – that according to the villager, was the nature of the rockslides.

'What should I do if I am caught in a rockslide?' I had asked the villager who looked like someone who had survived many rockslides. The response still rang in my ears. 'Once a few rocks start to fall, they have made a way. Once a few have made their way, others will follow. That is the nature of rocks. So, if you are caught in a rockslide, there is a rule in the mountains. MOVE. Either retrace your steps back or move forward. *Never stand still.*'

This was more than just a lesson in mountain climbing. This has remained with me as I climbed the mountain of life.

There were so many stories that I remember from my growing up which today serve as a compass for me to tide through the climbs and slopes. I would not be me if I did not have these stories. I would not be me if I had not had those years of deprivation of one kind or the other. *The only security was that there was no search for security*. Yet, yesterday's incident about my son betrayed how incomplete my parenting had been – that for something as small as this my son had to depend on me.

The worry was not that he needed me, the bigger worry was that I thought he would need me.

What a waste all those years growing up in the mountains have been! I have given my son resources but not resourcefulness; and sadly, in the process of giving him enough I have deprived him.

The thoughts continued to weigh heavy on me as I went down for breakfast. I did not talk to anyone that morning and no one disturbed me thinking that I was still shocked by the previous evening's play of events.

Throughout my journey I have gone with the flow without too much of planning, barring once when I deliberately and consciously wanted something for myself and that is the only time I messed it up. I can honestly give the credit of how my journey has flowed so far to the Government of India's initiative to help people from the North East. I am definitely a beneficiary of it, although in my mind at least I have worked hard too. If it would not have been for that help, I don't think I would have been able to overcome the limitations of my upbringing or the lack of facilities in the village I grew up.

My son today is a big votary of meritocracy and is against all kinds of reservations, little knowing that his father benefited from such schemes and if today he is able to argue against it so passionately then he must thank the very policies he is criticising.

I find his arguments against such privileges lacking perspective and a complete lack of knowledge of how people like us have lived our lives. I also believe it is my failure that he does not have the sensitivity to understand this. I had hardly spoken to him about my struggles because I never thought it was necessary. It was my past and it was behind us. He deserved the best and that best included not knowing the unfairness and ugliness of life. Our protectiveness towards our children often stunts their understanding of life.

People in privileged positions must expose their children to realities that exist beyond their drawing rooms or else they run the risk of raising armchair activists on meritocracy.

Often those who argue most vociferously in favour of meritocracy do so standing on the shoulders of generations of privileged lives.

The five years I spent in Delhi University were an eye opener – that I was different from others and being different was sometimes a reason enough for a lot of ridicule. I was 'chinki' to many, 'bahadur' to others and Sitam to only a few. I hear many in my circle of friends express anger at the racism they experienced in the countries they visited but they don't find anything wrong in name-calling me.

I understood student politics deeply and realised that hostels in a large university are no less than political theatres theatre. Everything plays out strongly – caste, religion, region, class, nepotism... you name it and it's there. I was of course not prepared for it. Most things did not bother me, but the very regular jibe at my North-Eastern looks and occasionally calling me Chinese did peeve me. Today I smile at it when I look back, but then my blood used to boil.

I knew I was an outsider at DU – but not in the way I was made to feel. I mean, it could not could not have only been.. in the way I looked because people from all other parts also looked equally different – the South Indians, the Punjabis and the Goans and the tribals; why only pick on us?

Those were the years when everyone moved in homogeneous groups – the Jats were together, the Punjabis were a gang, hell, even the Biharis moved in groups. It left no choice for us North-Easterners but also to create our own gang of comfort. I called it the ghettoization of Indian campuses. It did not appear abnormal to anyone and that surprised me. It was only many years later I figured out that human beings are fundamentally hardwired to remain in the ghettos of familiarity – and that familiarity did not stop at the way we looked; it included the way we thought and felt, it included the food we ate and songs we listened to and the language we spoke and of course the Gods we reached out to when life beat the shit out of us.

I enjoyed Confucius and Tao and many other Chinese philosophers, and it was no wonder that the 'Chinese' tag only became stronger. It is ironic that I am locked down because of a virus that emerged out of China or as the American President calls it – 'the Chinese virus'.

The only time I wanted to become something was when I wanted to qualify for the IAS so that I could reach a stage where all these voices that called out 'chinky' or 'Chinese' or 'Bahadur' would just not reach me. Of course, it is a different matter that is the only time I did not achieve what I so wished for, I ended up being a cog in the wheel of an extremely unromantic Indian bureaucracy, in the Ministry of Food and Supplies.

∞◇∞

It was around dinner time when the daily chit-chat resumed. Everyone shared their daily acquisition of news on Corona from across the world, mostly what is euphemistically called the WhatsApp university in many circles.

'What I like about this Corona thing, is that it is very secular. It is leaving no class of people untouched,' began Kulwant. 'The wife of the Canadian president tested positive, so did Prince Charles.

'I am told the English PM has also tested positive – is it true?' she further asked.

'There are three celebrities who have died – some Spanish princess died, and some German finance minister committed suicide,' said Razia. 'Why commit suicide?'

'Hope,' chipped in Sitam.

'Meaning?' asked Razia.

'Confucius says there are three things you need to be happy – love, work and hope. He seemed to have lost hope that things can be controlled or made better,' – explained Sitam.

'Are you saying that someone as powerful or influential as him lost hope?' Razia continued.

'Looks like that – one does not take the decision to take his own life so easily'. Sitam continued –

'We may go through tough times, but we largely bear it, sometimes with fortitude, at other times grudgingly – but taking our lives is a decision we would take when we have lost hope.'

'Interesting,' said Razia.

Sitam persisted with this line of thought, 'One thing that this Corona scare is definitely making clear – that in these moments most distinctions blur. The virus does not ask your religion – it is impacting Hindus and Muslims and Christians alike; it does not ask your riches – it is killing the poor and the prince alike; it is not asking your nationality – it is killing the Arabs and the Americans alike.'

'So much for all the fighting till only a few days ago all of them were having – where are those fights now? Everyone is shit scared and buried in their own holes,' commented Kulwant. 'Wish they could be like this all the time. Sometimes I feel it's good that they are scared – at least they are not fighting amongst each other.'

'We need toys to play all the time,' commented Sitam playfully.

'Meaning?' asked Kulwant

'Meaning, now the toy everyone is engaged with is the Corona. When it was not there, it was religion and race and class and nationality. These are toys we need to keep ourselves busy. It is easier to play with toys outside than deal with the voices inside.'

'That's the smartest thing you have said so far,' jibed Manoj, his tone betraying his smile.

Sitam ignored it. 'There are three methods to gaining wisdom. The first is reflection, which is the highest. The second is imitation, which is the easiest. The third is experience, which is the bitterest – Confucius again for all of you,' Sitam said dramatically and walked off towards the washroom.

Everyone wondered what did he really mean and who was this directed to?

6. The Stories of our End

Sunil Paswan

I can now speak English because it is my job to do so. However, anyone can figure out that it is not my natural language. The Bihari villager shows through. I have learnt it over the years, first by tuitions, and then through the local evening college. My hunger for progress will not be stopped by my not knowing English. I think and feel in Hindi though and that I do quite well.

Our end and the manner in which it shall come is the realm of philosophising at best and religiosity at worst. These days it is a matter unattended by both – because philosophising is a lost art and religion is about staying alive; God is just a means for seeking that extension of life.

I have always been haunted by the when and how of my end, and then what happens thereafter – these questions have never left me in all these years in Mumbai. The circumstances in which I came to Mumbai would never allow me to forget these questions.

I have always wondered at what precise point will I recognise that my end is near – that I am now meant to wither away, as a body and as a memory. I have always wondered at what precise point will I come face to face with the prospect of my end – dying at best and decaying at worst?

I wonder about the stories of all other men and women who have walked on the face of this earth, the thinkers and the doers, the non-thinkers and the non-doers, the high and mighty and the loners and the good for good-for-nothings – and I wonder about them; and I wonder as to when was it that they acknowledged the question of their end. Did they achieve something before or after this thought occurred to them that their time is limited here?

Did people start nourishing their greatness oblivious to the thought of being dead or do they increase their efforts and passion towards making this world a better place once they realise that that they are not going to be here forever?

I wonder, when will I become conscious of this question? Will it be only after I witness death, injury or sickness – when this question usually becomes pronounced when we return from a hospital or a funeral pyre. Some would see tragedies up close and personal and some would hear about it and become conscious of it. Some would see their own sugar levels soaring, lipid levels going berserk and blood pressure becoming uncivilised – and then ask, 'how will I go?'

I wonder if all of us see that mortality is as ubiquitous as air – unseen yet there. It is around every corner we turn, it's at the end of every breath we take. I wonder if the act of living is a delusion, a mass delusion at that, a myth humanity has built, cascaded and reinforced because it makes the pretence of living easy.

I wonder how others deal with the contradiction between the delusion of life and the certainty of its end. Maybe it is easier for the saints, the philosophers and the wise. I wonder how it is for those who have EMIs, jobs, and the monthly pressure of responsibilities. I wonder about those who realise the essential ephemerality and those who don't.

And finally, I wonder, what happens when such thoughts have been entertained? How do people react to these questions? I wonder what people do when they recognise the fragility of it all – the fragility of the strength of the bones and muscles, the fragility of their ability to walk, breathe and eat; the fickleness of speech, hearing and thinking?

I wonder if we have even the slightest clue about the unimaginable burden of a heart which cannot speak, the unimaginable grief of the limbs which cannot carry the body anymore.

I wonder about those who struggle to come to terms with it and I wonder about those who carry on with grace and courage. I wonder about the grammar of courage itself in the face of decay and death and what makes some courageous enough to look squarely in the eyes of the impending end without remorse or regret – and I wonder if at all there is a soul who can do this.

I know everyone shall eventually come face to face with this question. That day, there won't be ready answers, academic answers, or answers that have been bequeathed to us – that day, perhaps is the only day when we shall have 'our personal answer'. Education, erudition and sophistication will matter little on that day. I wonder what mine is. *The burden of life's end shall be borne lightly only by those who have taken the privilege of living itself lightly. For the rest it's going to be a burden.*

There is a reason why I keep thinking about the matters of my end even when I am very happy and want to live long.

I was born in a small village in the district Ara of Bihar. My father was a farm labourer who used to work in the fields of one of the rich farmers in the village belonging to a higher caste. Villages in Bihar, like the villages of many parts of the country, particularly during those times, were different from Mumbai or other cities. They are a different world. The big questions there are who can you talk to, who can you eat with, whose home you can go to, which parts of the village you can roam about, which girl can you see, which girl can you marry, who can you complain against – and the answers to all these questions are pre-decided. These things have been decided hundreds of years ago. I don't know who decided them, but they have been decided. Even talking about changing these things, leave aside actually changing them, is the first sign of madness.

There were a few armies in my village – no, no, not the Indian army, but a few *senas*. The landlords had one *sena*, the communists had one *sena*, the upper castes had one *sena* and we were left with no choice but to have one *sena* for ourselves. Everyone was a part of some *sena* or the other.

Everyone was armed, sometimes with guns but most of the times with anything sharp enough to wound or kill. Everyone paid allegiance to some *sena* if they had to survive and live. People still died – but at least you died belonging to something rather than being butchered without belonging to anyone. *There is only one thing worse than dying – that is dying for nothing.*

When you belong to some *sena* you represent something – in our village either you represented power, or you represented revolt. You had to let it be known. *It became easier to protect yourself this way and more importantly it became easier to kill this way.*

There was no rhyme or reason as to when one *sena* will attack the other. If the powerful did not like the way of celebrating your weddings, they would attack you. If you wore good clothes, they would attack you. If you asked for more wages, they would attack you. Basically, they would attack you as and when they felt like attacking you. So, what would you do – well soon you would attack them in return.

However, there was a difference. You attacked them in the dark while they attacked you in broad daylight. The difference was this – they felt entitled to their violence against us, while even in our courage to retaliate we needed the cover of the dark. Their violence was legitimate in their eyes, ours was not in our own eyes. *That is what thousands of years of discrimination does to you – it enters your bones; it corrodes your soul. It makes even your fight for justice feel illegitimate.*

I wanted to change things of course. No – that was not the problem. The problem was I wanted to change things in broad daylight. I started to raise questions about equal rights and access and many other things which had not been asked for thousands of years. Matters came to light when a fight broke out between the local high caste landowner's son and me in the school. It was a petty fight – the nonsensical reasons why boys in school fight. The schoolteacher somehow pulled us apart. I thought the matter was closed. However, it wasn't.

You see my name had a Paswan after it and his name had a Singh after it. In those days when a Paswan fought with a Singh, it was not about two young boys fighting over some petty matter in school. It was two communities fighting. It was the notion of honour fighting. It was much more than who fought with whom – what was important was who will put whom in his rightful place. Otherwise they feared that these things will go out of hand. Justice there is not understood the same way Justice is understood in Mumbai. Ara had its own courts and laws.

If during school the Paswan boy had hit the Singh boy, in the evening the Singh adults beat the Paswan adults!

Justice was swift and equal. By the time night fell, a *sena* representing the Paswans burnt the crops of the Singhs and thereafter began the spiral of violence in the village. Soon there were acres of burnt fields, loss of livelihood, half a dozen dead and many dozen injured. A government enquiry was commissioned, and the madness was traced to a young Sunil Paswan fighting with a young Singh boy in school.

My father convinced me to run away to a distant relative in Mumbai with a promise never to return to the village. It has been about 30 years and I have not returned. Mumbai and Hotel Landmark have been home ever since.

Life has been very good to me. I love this job. I get to interact with all kinds of people, who do not bother about my surname. You have no idea how liberating it was in the early days when no one asked me about my caste.

I meet people who are often richer, smarter and better than me. Yet I don't feel second to anyone. I don't think they can even compare what I have gone through and still reached where I have reached. I don't think I am arrogant – I think it is a huge advantage when you realise that you have raised yourself up from the bottom of the pit and so the fear of falling any further does not exist. I also know people who become too fearful of losing what they had acquired but I am the other kind. In my head I am still battling the same Paswan-Singh fight and surviving every day. Everything else has been easier thereafter. Of course, I don't share all of this with my wife or my son. This is my burden to carry.

I miss my village. I miss it for a variety of reasons but the most important of them is that I had an identity there. I am a nobody here. I was a doorman a few years earlier and I am the manager of Hotel Landmark now. Outside Hotel Landmark I am a nobody. There, I was Sunil. I was my father's son. I was a Paswan. I was of that village. And if nothing else I was from the district Ara. I had so many identities to fall back upon. Here, I am nobody.

My son does not get it. My son does not get that roots are important. It is the beginning of the formation of identity. The ties of place, kinship, family tree give us the overarching shade of a shared past – some kind of a banyan tree which helps us feel anchored. We do not float unanchored – we have something to hold on to – for whatever it is worth. Despite everything that identity brought on to me, I miss that identity. I miss the fact that I belonged.

I want to take him to my village where he can possibly trace the memories of a hundred years. He might meet only a few mud walls, maybe only a small room with a thatched roof, maybe ruins – but this would be the exact place, where once life flourished and which in a very philosophical way has been a precursor to my and his being. Hopefully, he will appreciate life more when he shall see how ruins look like. I wonder if I will ever go back to my roots. *I wonder if it is worth dying anywhere else apart from where you were born.*

At dinner Sunil Paswan joined his guests checking their comfort so far. Everyone started to share their woes with the hotel.

'The network is patchy,' said Manoj.

'The bathroom is not cleaned,' said Kulwant.

'Wish the food had more South Indian dishes,' complained Razia.

'There is no coke for Old Monk – Pepsi is too sweet,' smiled Sitam.

Everyone else smiled too. He offered the Old Monk to everyone. Interestingly with the exception of Kulwant everyone agreed. That surprised Sitam but soon he returned with an unopened Old Monk.

'I never imagined you would drink,' Said Manoj to Razia.

'That's because I am a woman, or I am Muslim?' asked Razia, in a tone that took Manoj aback.

'You people don't drink right – it's kind of haram or something like that?' said Manoj.

'What do you mean by YOU PEOPLE?' now Razia was getting impatient. 'What kind are us? We dropped from above, we came from outside or we mutated?'

'I did not mean that' Manoj almost stammered because his deepest thoughts had been betrayed.

'Let me not take offence Manoj – if I do, then Old Monk

will take offense,' said Razia, thawing the awkward moment.

'Well said,' remarked Sitam as he started to pour into glasses.

'Will you have one drink, Sunil?' asked Sitam.

Sunil was taken aback. He was not used to guests offering him a drink. He was a provider of convenience, but he understood his role was to be in the margins. He was like a painting that hung so that the room looked beautiful, but it does not mean the painting has to be hugged while sleeping. Sunil had spent his life being at the margins, being of utility and serving. He was not used to sitting at the table, being included, being served. Only a man so deprived in his soul will understand the shock such an invitation can elicit.

Sunil remained quiet. Sitam asked him again and this time with a little insistence. Sunil agreed 'Ok sir, a small one.'

Sitam passed on a glass to everyone. As they clinked their glasses, they realised that this was the first time they were attempting to forge something deeper than what had existed so far. So far, they were just strangers who through sheer happenstance were marooned together.

Human beings fundamentally don't like forming relationships, contrary to what they might tell themselves. They are either born in a relationship, which then they carry like a burden, not knowing what to do with it – or they create it for the purpose of fulfilling their physical needs. Rest all are relationships with a purpose – they fulfil some purpose, some transaction.

These five still did not know each other and their stories and their fears, they were still mere acquaintances trying to warm up to each other. They hoped desperately that Old Monk would help.

Captivity does this. We spend a lifetime with people without a genuine interest in knowing them. There is always an escape. There was no escape here. Proximity is a necessary condition for building a close relationship. When you are free, forging a relationship is a choice based on many factors, but in captivity it is enough to be a human being.

Our expectations during normal times with people and friendship is that there must be good vibes, there must be a match of standards, maybe a need for some common ground. Expectations change when you are in isolation and captivity. You search for a common ground – and if God forbid you don't get any, you give a damn.

Sunil was elated because he was on the table now as an equal. If only the others knew what that meant to him. It had taken a virus scare, a government lockdown and 4 strangers in captivity to make him feel equal and included.

Razia had felt angry and irritated with the insinuations of Manoj. She had hated and continues to hate labels like woman and Muslim, but they don't leave her alone. One cannot escape some labels.

Manoj was trying to be at ease with this motley group. He was uncomfortable since the first day because they were quite different from the kind of people he was used to interacting with. In his mind he was above them and their tastes. He could not help feeling superior.

Kulwant was lost. A party with strangers was yet another first she could tick off on her items during this trip.

Sitam was happy because he was not drinking alone.

Kulwant was observing the banter when her phone rang. She stepped out and returned with the colour from her face gone. Everyone became silent. They asked her what was wrong. She remained silent for a very long time – as if still evaluating if she should share what she had just come to know.

'Police had come to my house in Amritsar. They have put a poster of quarantine outside my home – asking no one to come out for the next 14 days.'

'Anyone suspected of having an infection?' asked Manoj.

'No. They are doing this for those who have returned from abroad in the last few days,' replied Kulwant.

'So, it is being done as a precaution. Nothing to worry. Everyone returning on an international flight is being quarantined. Relax,' Manoj tried to comfort her.

'No – that is not what I am thinking about,' murmured Kulwant.

'According to the police my husband returned from Bangkok – he had told us that he was going to Kolkata for a business trip!'

7. Of Summers and Rains

Kulwant was at that stage of her life where it was difficult to shock her. After a certain age life loses its ability to surprise us. It is the young who are surprised by the way life behaves. Youth believes life will follow the script; the old know better. They are surprised only when it indeed follows the script.

So Kulwant, contrary to her own expectations, was not surprised that her husband had gone to Bangkok – or why he would hide it from her. She wanted to feel hurt and betrayed but she could not. Her sense of anguish was not emerging from any personal let down. She knew what it meant for a man to go to Bangkok alone without telling his family. She was more worried about what the neighbours would say or think.

Another thing about old age is that personal hurt pales in comparison to public shaming – and beyond a certain age even that ceases to matter.

She knew that as she was getting used to the solitude and obscurity of Hotel Landmark – phones and messages would be cranking up in her locality in Amritsar. Juicy details would be getting exchanged. The town would have something new to occupy itself with. The Golden Temple is good for a while but the whole day is too long to be consumed happily by religiosity – one needed the spice of gossip. *Religion can satisfy the issues of the next life, but you still needed small talk to take care of this life.*

Kulwant was already afraid of returning to Amritsar and facing everyone, forgetting quite easily that it was only the sixth day of the lockdown.

Our fears do not follow a rule – sometimes what lies way ahead in the future torments us more than what lies right here.

She was not able to hate her husband even in this moment. She wondered why. Maybe life had taught her that we have exactly the same weaknesses that we condemn in others – our spouses included. *We often fight not because we are very different from each other but because we are all more or less the same.*

What irritates us about others is often a part of us only; we recognise the evil, the vile, and the mean in others only when we have all of this in us aplenty.

Conflict is integral in relationships. All conflicts begin with the humble and innocuous difference of opinions. There are some conflicts that remain as difference of opinions while others become monstrous over time – adding layers of hurt, real or imagined, threats to identities, the insatiable hunger for power and the helpless need to be one up.

When two people do not get along well and continue to fight, it is really fascinating to find out what is making them invest so much of themselves to keep the fight alive.

Keeping a hurt alive is a full-time job. It demands so much of us. It demands that we simmer with that hurt at all times, keeping the flames of all the past memories at high sim lest the hurt gets cold. This is easier to do when the two are very similar rather than too different from each other.

It is fascinating to observe the conflicts between the different strands of the same religion as against between two very different religions, or conflict between two parts of the same country as against between two different countries, or conflict between two people very close to each other as against between two strangers – the former in all these cases is always more vicious and bitter.

I guess the conflict between two people close to each other is acuter and more ferocious because both know each other too well. The knowledge of where things hurt is better and so the blow, when it is delivered, is done so for maximum impact.

The hurt is the gravest because it was someone close. Strangers do not hurt us because we are not invested in them.

There is one more reason which is the most hideous of all, most painful – that the hurt emerges from an anger that we have with ourselves; it's just that the manifestation is directed outwards. In the experience of pettiness, vileness, cunningness, meanness of others and in witnessing the ability of others to be vengeful and remorseless – we are reminded that we too have them in us. We know that we are no better than what we are at the receiving end of.

In that fleeting moment when our own lies get exposed, where we become aware of our imperfections, we do not know how to redeem ourselves. Anger is our only recourse – and that anger is directed outside. The higher our disappointment is with ourselves, higher is the manifestation of that anger outside.

The fire that burns inside the blade of grass often ends up burning the forest.

Kulwant was swept over by a cloud of thoughts. How should she deal with this, she wondered? Should she react, fight and make a scene as she knew she was entitled to and capable of, or should she just let the storm pass?

She knew of only two ways of dealing with pain and hurt, of which there have been many instances in her rather long life. She could be the *Stoic* – deal with such pain or at least put a brave face on it, or she could be a *Sponge* – absorb the enormity of the emotion deeply and completely.

The moment we start analysing our grief we have started to overcome it. The pain that we do not understand or are unable to describe or analyse, is the one that makes us suffer the most.

Stoics are better she thought – at least there appears a calm around them. They seem to be above human agony. Moving away from people in whom you have invested your most vital part – your time, can result in a huge sense of loss. An investor who has lost money on an asset becomes a recluse on all investing. It's not that a particular investment has gone wrong; in a way it's the act of investing itself which has gone wrong.

She wondered how the stoics could overcome this. She had ended up becoming part cynic and part admirer of the stoics – cynic because she was growing to believe they were fakes and admirer because she knew in her heart, she wanted to be like them.

As a child she was in awe of the strength of parents, intelligence of teachers and the aura of importance elders carried – she grew up to know that it was facades in most cases and fake in some.

There was a part of her that believed that stoics were imposters like all of them, waiting to be exposed.

Yet in other moments she liked the sponges more than the stoics. She marvelled at the magnanimity with which sponges absorbed everything that came their way – sometimes to the extent that the sponges acquired the nature of what they were absorbing. Those who absorbed longing and ache of the heart started to look like that anguish; 'But at least they are authentic,' she counter argued.

She was in awe of the sponges too. She knew that sponges allowed experiences to enter every pore, every sinew, every part of their being.

She was envious of the sponges because she felt that they knew the unbridled joy of being in love, the sharp hurt in the middle of the chest when the heart breaks, the dark abyss of hopelessness that stares you during a separation, the sleeplessness that comes calling, the absolute loss of zing from the act of living even when practically everything is intact.

The sponges knew all of it because they did not run away from feeling anything. They were allowing life to happen to them as purely in agony as much in unbridled joy!

She was arguing on both sides. She did not know if she was a stoic or a sponge. She oscillated like a pendulum. The pendulum however is its own prisoner. It is important for the pendulum to realise that while it is its ambition to stretch from one extreme to another, while it must stretch its hands farthest to grab something that lies just a shade beyond where its reach ends – it is its destiny to be pulled back to the opposite end just as strongly.

The pendulum must realise that its destiny is swinging from one extreme to another – not in trying to touch the extremes. Her question though remained unanswered – whenever the pendulum realises the dark helplessness of its existence, will it deal with it like a stoic or like a sponge?

Sunil Paswan felt it was his duty to share the state of the world and the latest news in his typical *bhel puri* fashion – particularly after he had broken bread, or rather Old Monk yesterday with everyone.

'It's becoming worse. I thought it would stop with this lockdown. The numbers in India have crossed 1000 with 27 already dead.'

'And don't even talk about the world; there are more than 31,000 dead and surprisingly the numbers infected in USA are more than China,' he continued.

'Where are you from Mr Paswan?' – asked Razia.

'Bihar, madam,' Sunil replied respectfully.

'Who else is there?'

'Uncles are there. Parents are long dead. There is a younger brother, but he works as a labourer in Delhi, at a construction site. I tried getting him here, but he cannot work in one place for more than a few weeks. Every family drama has one casualty madam – in our case it was my brother,' Sunil described, happy at the thought that he was answering a simple question in quite a sombre fashion.

'Do you miss home?' asked Razia

'I don't miss home – but I do miss the summers there.'

'The summer of Mumbai is not same madam,' began Sunil Paswan.

'Summer in my village, away from the cool indulgence of the mountains or the moderating caress of the shores, is oppressive. I never found it oppressive then – there was poetry in even the heat. It had its own rhythm, its own festivity, its own celebration.

'The mornings would take birth in the ever-cool flowing waters of the stream nearby and by 10.00 the world would start to recede back into the shades. The charpoy beneath the mango tree would come out for a few hours. The sunlight would shimmer through the thick maze of leaves, not tormenting but present – the heat not yet violent but threatening to be so. The crows and the cuckoo would be active in fairly loud conversations without a care for who might be eavesdropping.' It was as if Sunil was back in his village.

'Mother would offer thin buttermilk made from the slightly tangy curd of the night before. The afternoons would be a tussle between angry grandparents on one hand, who would want a reprieve from the long days – and the recalcitrant children who would want to use the peace to creative use. Tiptoeing to sneak out to go back to the fields, climb up trees or do absolutely nothing was a daily adventure – many times getting caught red handed, after which it would be difficult to ascertain what contributed to hot cheeks more, the weather or the slaps.

'The evenings were often long hours of running in the dry fields which would now be open to alternative uses before the next crop is sowed. Playing indigenous games in the rough terrain of erstwhile paddy fields is an experience difficult to imagine for those who have not done it. Marbles were played with gusto. The joys of kite flying would only be matched by the joy of the process of making the kites and sharpening the threads.

'The wilderness around villages has much benevolence – the roads, fields and the desolate lands is laden with tamarind, custard apple, jujube, jamun, and indigenous varieties of mangoes. Summer was associated with our band of vagabonds going in search of these, aim at the fruits with stones and then admire our own accuracy as the fruit would fall down. The spoils would always be shared. Sometimes the tree would belong to some household and hence the entire act would acquire the seriousness of a covert operation – a kind of surgical strike in the middle of the hot afternoon when everyone would be sleeping. For the longest time I thought mangoes are to be sucked rather than cut and eaten because of the ones we got there – thin peeled, juicy and syrupy.

'Summer nights would often also be absolutely still but starry. The roofs would become community bedrooms and on those still nights when even whispers would sound stereophonic, the children would giggle helplessly and without reasons.

'There is great joy in community laughter particularly when the only reason is to irritate parents who want you to sleep. Mosquitoes added to the charm. No one had yet heard of dengue, chikungunya and having malaria was like an annual pilgrimage – everyone had it.

'Summer then was a season that I experienced like life, with all its folly and all its prickliness. I experience the summer now from a distance, as if it's someone else's summer. My summer is lost. Not sure if I will ever get it back – and even if I do get it, I am not sure if I will enjoy it as much,' finished Sunil Paswan.

'You speak of your village very differently Mr Paswan,' said Razia. Clearly something in the manner that Sunil had spoken had touched her.

The uniqueness about human stories is that the details may differ but essentially, they are the same. The differences evaporate when you cut through the drama and experience the core of it.

Razia belonged to the other end of the country from Sunil Paswan, belonged to a different culture and religion, a different worldview and yet there was something in the manner in which he described the summer of his childhood and his village that touched her – she felt his summer was familiar or her own; most importantly, it made her reminisce her relationship with her village and its seasons.

'Your summers may have been special Mr Paswan, but the king of seasons is clearly the rains – and that too in Kerala,' Razia said, warmly and perhaps a little boastfully.

'Why do you say that madam' asked Sunil.

Razia began. 'You see Mr Paswan, summer is oppressive overall. The heat burns the skin and the eyes and even after sundown you feel the earth throwing back the heat in anger for its torment during the day – the air is sucked dry of its life and vitality. Trees maintain a brave face, tendrils have their backs broken, stray animals become introverts – and humans search for islands of shade, cool and air-conditioning, depending upon what they can afford.

'I have seen some winters in the north – and I can say they are dull and depressing overall. The fog and the overcast skies hang like a pall of gloom right before a catastrophe or right after it. The lack of sun and brightness is not only the state of the world but in a strange way also the state of the soul – as if someone has robbed us of the shine from us, as if we have watched an infinitely depressing movie. The sartorially experimental enjoy winters for what they could flash and show off but in many ways that is actually an attempt to compensate for the lack of brightness within and around.'

'What's your point madam?' asked Sunil.

'My point is – that at a very aggregate level, both summers and winters are takers not givers. However, Rains are special. Rains are like grandparents – infinitely large hearted and net givers.

'As the skies shower their benevolence upon us, the first reaction is of relief. The first rains are a balm for the earth and its inhabitants, comforting the blisters that they had acquired through the many months of summer. The first rains are therapeutic for they teach us to hang on just a few more weeks through the torment and oppression of the summers. That is a lot like life.

'As the clouds change colour and flirt with the sun, we pick up playfulness from the weather. Rains are not like the constant hammering of the furnace of summer or the constant bite of the chill, but they are like the game of a child – sometimes the tease of a drizzle, sometimes the unimaginative cadence of a snore, and sometimes the aggression of a heavy downpour.

'There is an innate unpredictability in rains, a refreshing contrast with the utter constancy of the characteristics of the summers and winters. Rains are playful and flirty like an adolescent romance. It hurts sometimes but mostly it is warm and mushy – and for no reason at all it adds a spring to the steps and songs to the lips.

'Rains provide not only succour but also enable life to exist and flourish. There would be practically no food and life without rains. We owe life and its myriad manifestations to rains.

'The essential nature of rains is to be moderate. Regions that are lucky to have the bounty of rains usually pass on those characteristics to the life forms that live there. Deserts and frozen snowy peaks are extremes and pass on that ruggedness to the life forms that inhabit them.

Rains are a metaphor for abundance. Scarcity is the nature of the arid – both of the extreme hot and extreme cold type. The tropics are givers. The arid are hoarders.'

'Rains make you feel like going out and dancing like no summer or winter will ever be able to make you feel.

'Have you heard even one song on the summers or winters Mr Paswan?' Razia asked rhetorically.

'We don't go out to sing and dance in summers and winters – but we intuitively feel like dancing and singing in the rains, with the rains and for the rains – and I rest my case,' concluded Razia.

Someone was clapping – it was Manoj. Kulwant was smiling. Sitam was busy tearing into the chicken leg piece and Sunil Paswan was looking at her with his mouth agape.

It is surprising to see what a person can do in captivity. Razia and Sunil were talking about seasons as if they were two friends sitting in a park, as if life was normal. It was impossible to believe that these strangers were in captivity in a nationwide lockdown. All things that they had taken for granted only until recently were no longer there. All of them, despite their circumstances were still searching for small moments of happiness. It was hardly taking an effort from them – at least much less than what they would have suspected it would take.

Human nature is the most obstinate and the most flexible – we just don't know which one will kick in when.

8. Heretics, The Sikhs and The Taliban

Two things happened as the next day of the lockdown dawned in the country and in Hotel Landmark – and one of them ended up breaking the bonhomie that was just beginning to take shape between the four strangers and a manager. The day would end with all of them going back to their rooms absolutely sure that not only did they dislike many in the group but also sure that they would not like to see them ever again.

It began with Sunil reading out the news from the country and across the world to each one of them at the breakfast table. He had started to join the guests during the meals.

'You know, there was some masjid in Delhi, where there were hundreds of people assembled for some religious congregation, which the police had to forcibly vacate – there were many foreign nationals who had come. Many of them are infected. Now we don't know how many had attended this congregation. They have spread across the country,' opened Sunil.

'The whole social media is filled with stories about this,' added Sitam. He continued, 'Needless to say, this is no longer a health problem or a law and order problem – it is acquiring a Hindu-Muslim angle.'

Manoj jumped in. 'These people are like that only – they can do just about anything in the name of minority rights and the freedom to practice their religion; and dare anyone say anything to them or to their Gods.' His voice acquiring a foment by the second.

'You are being harsh and unfair Manoj,' Sitam tried to pacify.

'I am being unfair! Are you serious? Wake up Sitam. It's people like you who in the name of equal rights and human rights have created this problem. You have systematically weakened the actions that should have put such nonsense in its rightful place long ago. Nehru baked this drugged cake of secularism and for more than half a century everyone has eaten it without acknowledging its side effects. It was a small wound – you have allowed it to fester.'

'Come on Manoj – not Nehru again! He cannot be the source of all problems this country has – and for how long – just how long will you keep bringing up his name?'

'As long as it takes to solve the problems he created,' blurted Manoj. 'As long as these people do not realise that for long, they have taken the system for a ride.'

'And who are these people – I heard you say this the other day too,' – It was Razia. 'Are these people different from you, have they come from Mars, and what do you mean by putting them in their rightful place – I mean what is *my* rightful place?'

'I did not mean you,' said an irritated Manoj.

'But I am them – I share their religion and that label describes me too,' said Razia.

'The funny thing is till today I have rarely identified myself as a Muslim – as a woman yes, as a Malayali yes, but as a Muslim rarely. My religion was something I was born into – I may or may not share that religiosity. I have many disagreements with the way it is practiced. In fact, I am not even sure if I believe in God.'

Razia continued, 'But today when you talked about the Muslims as if it's a label – and by using it you have pulled me into it; by using that label you have left me with no choice but to forget that in my head I am woman first or a Malayali second – I am being reduced to only one label – my religion.

'....and given the tone of your voice, surely more menacing than you would care to admit, I am not left with any choice but to make being a Muslim my primary identity and worse still defend it,' Razia paused.

'You do not have a choice in that – that is the identity that everyone out there has, wants to continue with. They refuse to see all that is wrong in the way that religion is set up, is practiced, and all the wrong that is happening in the name of propagating or protecting that religion. People like us consume that and make our opinion. So do not give me this intellectual shit. Real life is about millions of people who think and behave a certain way and I will make my opinion based on that,' retorted Manoj.

Kulwant entered the debate. 'That may not be true Manoj – people make opinions even when they have no adequate reason to do so. They think like you even when there are no facts. You have all the facts that you are quoting from around the world as your reasons to believe that you are justified in seeing Muslims in the light that you are seeing – maybe many of those facts are true also. I can assure you that there is more to it than meets the eye – we need easy answers, easy scapegoats. We want enemies to pin the blame for all the woes around us. Remember the Sikh riots of 1984? None of your theories were true and yet that massacre happened!

'I must say this – be careful when you paint everyone with the same brush. Every time you do that ask yourself whose brush is it anyway? Who is making me paint everyone in the same colour – either as a hero or as a villain – the hand maybe ours but often they are someone else's colours,' continued Kulwant. 'And if it's a matter pertaining to religion, then it is even more likely to be so.'

'I must say Kulwant, I was reminded of my days as a student in the Delhi University – this word *'you people'* was often used about us. 'You people' eat snakes, dogs, cockroaches *kya*? You people can speak Hindi *kya*? *What the hell is 'you people'!*' butted in Sitam.

'I have since then developed a repulsion for this phrase. Don't mind Manoj, you will never understand the anguish of people who are addressed with the prefix – 'you people'. I think you sound quite prejudiced right now.'

'Prejudiced!' Manoj screamed. 'Look at all the acts of terrorism in almost all the parts of the world *and I am prejudiced*! Mine is what is called an informed opinion, Mister.'

'Prejudice often begins when you are certain – and so does stupidity,' this was Kulwant. 'I have often wondered what makes us so susceptible to draw such strong lines between people like us and people who are not like us.'

All the years in Kulwant were showing as she continued. 'I mean sometimes the number of lines that separate us are so many – religion clearly takes the cake in its ability to divide; *I mean God must have killed more than he would have saved I think.'*

'I am not sure if God is a person or an idea – and in all those hours I spend in the Golden Temple this thought does not leave me.

'I am not sure if he is someone to be loved or feared, I am also not sure if he is to be explored or revered. All I know is that he is too important to most of us, so important that we can go to any extreme in his name. I don't know if he Himself is mild or moderate in his temperament but I can very well see that as his followers we do not hesitate to go to extremes to protect his reputation from hurt, real or imagined.

'I don't know if he sees us all the time from some vantage point as many would like us to believe but I do know that we keep Him around us all the time. I don't know if He is jovial and fun loving and if He has fun doing His business of keeping this well-oiled machine called universe firmly in its place and its engines running, but I do know that his followers and disciples do lack a sense of humour.

'I don't know if He is accommodating or not but most of His followers certainly are not accommodating.

'I don't know if I was created by Him or whether he holds the strings to my destiny and hence it is advisable to be in His good books. I don't know if I should listen to the rationalists and believe only that which I can see and prove, or should I hear the merchants of faith who ask me to submit unquestioningly and let Him handle what is eloquently called my destiny. What I do know is that I fear bad outcomes and unfulfilled dreams and that I do not understand and cannot explain many things that happen around me. Inexplicability is fertile ground for faith to flourish. Fear creates conditions for search of an anchor. *Fear makes God possible.*

'Who is God and what role He plays in my life appears to be a metaphysical question on the one hand and an extremely practical question on another. I am confused if there is a My God and Your God and Other Gods; I am confused about the business of religion. Rituals that I grew up with, which were at the centre of the notion of God and which gave me comfort and succour till a while back are increasingly appearing meaningless. Should I worry about the scorns of the heavens?

'If God is an Experience as the mystics have said, that He reveals Himself only to the deserving, then I guess so far I am not deserving. I have had no such epiphany so far.

'I know this for sure – there is an innate need in each of us to want to believe in something bigger than us. In worshipping something spectacular we perhaps uplift ourselves too.'

Kulwant's long speech brought back some civility to the debate.

'You mean to say that whatever we see and read we should ignore? Dig a hole in the ground, put our head like an ostrich in it and believe that all is well in the world? How can you not see that it is a game to establish a world order – haven't you heard of the dreams of the caliphate?' asked Manoj.

'Use of power, either violent or not has never solved problems of belief and faith *sirjee,*' said Sunil Paswan. Everyone was taken aback. Here was an extremely deep argument between educated people happening. No one knew what exactly it was that took them by surprise – the fact that it was Sunil Paswan, a mere hotel manager of a lowly hotel or his uncouth Bihari accented language or their own expectation that such a person can even have an opinion on a subject such as this or his confidence to express it at this delicate stage. *Labels come in various forms. Those who defend the use of labels are often likely to use them.*

'It has been seventy years that India has been free. Come to my village and I will show you the hundreds of ways in which it is not. I have not returned to my village for more than 30 years because some upper-caste person thought that he had to punish my entire family and my caste because a small kid belonging to a lower caste had the temerity to fight with his son – that society could not digest two 16-year-olds fighting!

'We thought we could solve the problem of caste through violence – through countering one form of violence with another. We believed if we could instil sufficient fear in the perpetrators of the violence then they would stop. We couldn't though.

'Were we wrong – tell me, were we wrong in asking for our rights, our dignity and self-respect?' Sunil asked no one in particular.

'No, we were not wrong in that expectation. *We were wrong in the belief that it was violence.. that would bring us that respect.* Fact is – violence begets more violence. It's a never-ending spiral.

'Whoever is fighting these wars of religions also has to understand that.

'I am told things started to change in my village only when someone from our caste came to that area as District Collector some twenty years ago. It shocked people for many years and it was not easy for the rest to accept that the power structures had turned upside down. That was the turning point – many more came after that but most importantly it became easier for people to accept others as equals. I am hoping that 16-year-olds from different castes can now fight there without fearing for their lives and the lives of their entire family,' said Sunil and then became quiet.

Kulwant was back. It was difficult to ascertain if she was consoling Sunil or reprimanding Manoj or advising Sitam and Razia – '*Badi bahut dilchasp hai, hangama-khez hai; Neki kathin hai, lohe ke chane chabane ki tarah – wrote the famous author Ismat Chugtai'*

'It means bad is interesting, dramatically eventful; good is difficult, like chewing iron.'

'No wonder vice is a magnet that pulls us and sucks us into it. I am not sure what is the exact word for *'hangama khez'* in English – perhaps dramatically eventful – but it does not really capture the depth and imagery of the original Urdu word.

'Bad has the power to disrupt, to create ripples, to create flutter and a drama which has its own life. It has momentum and exhilaration, an ability to make things happen like nothing else. It engenders action, which is also immediate and urgent. It's difficult to resist it. It has a sway over us.

'Good rarely has that power. It's boring and drab. It might have many other virtues but good is rarely exciting. No wonder there are not many takers for it.

'The polarity of good and bad can be extremely unnerving and sometimes meaningless too.

'I am becoming more and more acutely aware that the right and the wrong change colours over time, sometimes they even change places – be careful about what you are certain to be good and right,' the emphasis was stronger this time from Kulwant.

'Let me share some interesting words and their original meanings,' it was Sitam who clearly wanted to lighten the mood a bit.

'What does the word heretic mean?' He waited for no one to answer and said, 'It means a person to have another opinion...'

'... and we used to kill heretics – we still do actually,' this time it was Manoj.

'Precisely – we killed people just for the crime of having a different opinion and the funny thing is we still do it. Wherever we cannot kill, we troll them on social media.

'Ok – let me ask the meaning of another word now that we are playing this game,' said Kulwant.

'What is the meaning of the word Sikh?' She also waited for no one and answered, 'It means a disciple, to learn. A good Sikh is a life-long learner. Now go and tell that to most Sikhs today that the real definition of a good Sikh is to be that, and you will know how much they really know their religion,' Kulwant sounded exasperated... almost.

'What does the word Taliban mean?' this time it was Razia who dropped the bomb.

No one dared to answer.

'It means to be the learned – the one who learns.'

9. On the Other Side Lies Happiness

More than a week away from home and family, with strangers, stuck in a hotel and nowhere to go! This is not something that any of the inmates of Hotel Landmark would have imagined as their idea of fun or holiday – and yes, they had definitely turned into inmates from being guests in many ways.

We often dream of good times and usually it is about taking a holiday, away from the humdrum of daily routine. Many of us even dream of solitude in the mountains and on beaches. Solitude is an idea that would have bewitched us all at some point or the other.

In fact, most ideas from a distance look very appealing. People living in democracies, particularly noisy and messy ones, look at benevolent authoritarianism with hopeful eyes. People living in dictatorships look at democracies and rue what they are missing. Theocratic states miss liberal dispensations and liberal states want to bring back the rule of the Lord. Singles miss families and those with families want to be single again.

Orphans miss parents and kids with parents find parents claustrophobic. Tropics miss the winters of the poles and those in the poles find themselves condemned to chilling winters. Young want to grow up fast and the old want to become children again. Those who have not found love miss the idea of it and those who are in love experience its dark sides.

The four inmates in Hotel Landmark on the eighth day of the lockdown were beginning to see the shades of life and the hollowness of their own desires more clearly now.

Sitam had always wanted to take rest. He was tired of running around, of trying to prove, of being the provider. He had dealt with the pressure of a small village boy wanting to make a place under the sun, achieve something and be a role model all his life. His achievements were not only his own but also of his extended family and his village and sometimes even for the people of the North East.

He had not wanted this, but some burdens are not for us to choose. They are thrust upon us. Soon you realise that your shoulders hurt carrying this load. No one sees or knows your demons, the nights you have burned holding that load over your head – they only see what is coming out, and they feel it was all easy for you. The real anguish is not that your burdens cannot be shared, the real pain is that even the story of that burden cannot be shared. There is no soul lonelier in this world than that.

Kulwant had always wanted to run away from being the responsible one. She was sick and tired of being the provider and the nourisher – the person who will be subsumed by the act of fulfilling the desires of others. She had to make sacrifices as a daughter, as a wife and as a mother. Her anguish was that it was assumed that she will make those sacrifices. Sure, all those roles were important for her and she derived meaning from fulfilling those roles – of being a loving daughter, wife and mother. All she hated was that it was assumed that she had no other wish, no other role she wanted to play and no other source of joy she wanted to nourish. *We are all prisoners of the roles we perform. After a while the role becomes our complete identity. It chokes. We are more than the sum of our roles.*

Razia was always free. She was perhaps looking for a purpose larger than herself. She wanted to have a life which had a meaning bigger than what she did for herself. She had all that she needed and wanted. However, she was floating – and her fear was that she would continue to float in the future too. She would wonder if she would be able to look back at her life and feel satisfied that it has been a life lived well enough.

Is our life a sum total of all our wants? Is a life so perfect even worth living? Razia always wanted to know what a life of imperfection means – a life where childhood has been a challenge or Maybe there has been no childhood, where shoulders and the soul droop carrying the burden of expectations, where unrequited love makes the heart create soul wrenching poetry. She had always wondered about the role of pain, melancholy and grief in shaping lives.

Manoj had always wondered what a life without a terrible urge to win would be like – where there was no pressure on him to be the best. He wanted to know what it was to be normal, not be the best, not have the last word and always win an argument. He admitted that he enjoyed winning and being the best – it gave an adrenaline rush to him, it made running the race worth it.

However, he was increasingly realising that not every time he won, he felt victorious. The instances, where the joy he derived from winning an argument or a debate or an assignment at work was not commensurate to the size of his victory were increasing. He could not understand it, but he knew. *He knew many times that even when he had won, he had actually lost.* However, he was too proud to admit it.

He wanted to know what it meant to take it easy, to not have a schedule, a tight time calendar for the day, a day filled with 10 things to be achieved, a day and life which is a prisoner of the watch. He did not remember such a day ever existing for him – for this is the only way he has known life to be. Even his relationships were governed by the watch – this hour for the children and that hour for the wife! He used to get jittery if the time slots in his mind got changed or extended. All his life, he had thought that this precision and clockwork was a virtue. Time, he preached, is a resource that needs to be preserved.

Manoj did not know the power of being in the flow, or the magic of spontaneity. He always wondered how his life would be when he will not have a list of things to do. He had been scared of this prospect and here he was, in Hotel Landmark, reaching that stage. He was petrified.

Sunil had lived his life with the singular task of surviving. He did not remember a day since he'd left his village where he was able to even think of what he wanted for himself. His needs were clearly survival – first to have enough food and a shelter in a city like Mumbai. More importantly, he did not ever want to go back to the situation that he had to run away from. He had grown to detest the idea of being at the mercy of others, particularly those who were more powerful than him. He had grown to loathe those who had certain privileges since birth and who used those privileges to scare others. He had promised himself that he will remain free. All that he sought from life was the freedom of the soul – it was okay if he had less money and no house and all the other things that people found satisfaction in owning – *all he wanted was never to be owned by another human being.*

In Hotel Landmark that day everyone had reached a point where they were thinking – really thinking. They realised that they had not thought deeply for a long time. They realised that life had a funny way of sucking you into matters of survival and responsibilities. It robbed us of the most important faculty that made us special in the first place – the ability to pause and reflect.

In going through the pause, they also came to the realisation that they had forgotten how to slow down – this they found extremely discomforting. Slowing down can be disturbing. Pausing and reflecting on such things can be scary. Reflection needs practice and life often does not allow us that practice. One has to steal those moments. *They realised that reflection has to be budgeted for – otherwise it will slip down in the order of priorities and soon that ability will get rusted.*

Each of them was also disturbed.

Sitam realised that for him the matter of identity had been touchy because of all the taunts and jibes he faced during his days at DU.

Razia realised that she was touchy on matters of being labelled.

Kulwant realised that her wounds of the failed love affair still hurt her after all these years and the Hindu-Muslim fault-line reminded her that the world had not changed even a small bit.

Manoj realised that he had something against Muslims subconsciously, and Sunil realised that he was still the young boy who was running away from the fight in his village in Bihar.

We might leave our battlegrounds, but our battles rarely leave us.

Manoj was reading a book while having breakfast.

'Are you seriously into reading?' asked Kulwant.

'What exactly does that mean Kulwant?' asked Manoj.

'In my opinion, there are genuine readers and then there are readers who read just so they can talk about the fact that they are reading something,' Kulwant's tone was clearly warm with the intention of having some fun. Luckily it was understood and reciprocated by Manoj.

'How many kinds of readers do you know of?' he asked her.

'Many!'

'Tell me about a few.'

'Well, I can think of two that I have seen, and I hate them both,' began Kulwant.

'There are the *Imposters,*' smiled Kulwant, 'they always carry a book and that is the only thing one can be sure of; that they are *carrying* it. Reading, for them is more a status symbol, an act of wannabe intellectual – the same reason why they would not wear just a suit but only an Armani or carry not just a bag but only a Louis Vuitton!'

'You know how I deal with the Imposters?' asked Kulwant.

'How?' asked Manoj – he was liking this side of Kulwant's.

'Take your revenge – just ignore the book and refuse to have a conversation around it. It will frustrate them to no end,' she was almost giggling.

'And the second kind?'

'Ah, the second kinds are the *Worms.*'

'What about them?'

'Irrespective of the title they are reading, which might range from the tapeworms in your bowels to the climate change in Mars – they are immersed in it as if they are praying. The book is larger than their persona. They are also barring you from beginning any conversation with them. I can almost predict that these kinds have relationship issues with human beings – but saying that can be highly controversial, isn't it?'

Manoj was in splits by now. He had underestimated the old Punjabi woman from Amritsar – in the astuteness of her observations and her crackling sense of humour. Others were around and enjoying the banter between two very unlikely people. They were also pleasantly surprised by Manoj's ability to have a light-hearted conversation like this.

'Let me share a third type, Kulwant, and let's see if others can think of other kinds of readers,' he said obviously trying to get others also involved in this.

'I can think of the *Flirts.*'

'Flirts? How can readers be flirts Manoj?' almost exclaimed Kulwant, part laughing and part shy of the usage of the word flirt.

Manoj began, 'As the name says it all, these readers flirt with books, they suffer from commitment phobias. No book can hold their attention for more than a few pages. All books, according to them, have a problem. Some are too boring, some too long, some have font problems, some have weight problems, and some that them have no pictures!'

Kulwant was laughing without restraint by now, holding Sitam's arms for support.

'Anyone else know of any other kinds of readers?' Asked Manoj and looked around.

'Let me try,' said Razia – '*The Show-offs* – I gather you would be one of them,' it was banter and surprisingly Manoj either did not get the sarcasm or he just let it go given the moment.

'The Show-offs actually read the book, less to immerse and enjoy but to let you know that they have actually read the book. All conversations will be veered towards that book irrespective of the moment or the occasion. You will have to politely tolerate the absolute irrelevance of book to the mood. The revenge with the show-off is to talk about an even more irrelevant book than the one he is reading!'

Everyone was in splits by now.

'I know of another category, the *Rebels,*' joined in Sitam.

'The Rebels cannot understand how a normal human being can spend so many precious hours of human life so frustratingly tied up with something hopeless and boring such as a book. The Rebel believes that all the books that were supposed to be read have already been read from KG to the 10th – everything else must be rebelled against. The

Rebel believes real education happens on the streets and not on the couch.'

'You know, a writer friend of mine says that he does not read books because they interfere with his imagination. I have not asked him so far whether his books will interfere in the imagination of others – remember he is a friend after all!'

'I must add one type I know,' emerged the voice of Mr Sunil Paswan.

Everyone fell silent suddenly and then erupted in laughter as they awaited the earthly humour of Sunil

'These kinds of readers are called *The Occasionals*. The Occasional reads roughly one book a year and for precisely the same reason why the diehard non-vegetarians keep the *Navratra* fast – as a hollow show of penance.'

Hotel Landmark amidst the gloom and doom of COVID-19 and on the eighth day of the lockdown was a very happy oasis. *It also became very clear it, often does not take much to create warmth, just as it often does not take much to create animosity.*

10. Walk till you are Home!

It was difficult to ascertain whether they overslept for no apparent reason or they did it because yesterday ended on a happy note, but most of them came down late that morning.

Everyone had their own way of consuming news which they were busy reading while having breakfast. They would have read that while they were having their banter here in Hotel Landmark oblivious to the crises outside, India witnessed the largest spike in the number of COVID detection at 370, taking the total detection to 1637 with 38 deaths. Across the world the number was kissing a million and people were dying of it. America had long overtaken China in terms of the numbers of cases detected, Italy and Spain were struggling and so was Iran. India appeared a non-issue in comparison to their numbers – at least so far.

This was also the time they should have realised that those who do not watch TV or read a dozen news sites and consume WhatsApp as a source of information were most likely to be positive and joyous, otherwise one was sure to believe that the world was coming to an end. They were not fortunate enough to have that realisation.

They would have also noticed that many unprecedented things were happening. The Wimbledon was postponed, the only time after the World War II – except that this time more than 180 countries out of the 190 odd were either infected or under serious threat in comparison to the World War which was fought by only a dozen countries.

In the pall of doom that was descending they would have noticed that the Indian corporate sector was opening its purses to be of help. Finally, only the truly optimistic would have noticed that it was the ninth anniversary of India winning the cricket World Cup in 2011.

In the last few days they would have also read about lakhs of migrant workers lining up to return home, thereby making a mockery of the lockdown, social distancing and the government preparation. However, none of them would have thought much about it. They were too far removed from the woes of migrant workers.

It was left to Sunil Paswan to raise it.

'Do you miss your homes?' he began harmlessly.

'What kind .. kind of a question is that Mr Paswan?' asked Kulwant. 'Of course, we do!'

'I mean what exactly do you miss about your homes – do you miss the building, the family or the city or its people – what specifically do you miss about not being at home?'

'That is a deep one,' admitted Sitam.

'I miss comfort, the assurance that I know where exactly things are and that I will get what I need even with my eyes closed,' commented Manoj.

'I miss my family the most – the noise and clutter of my children, the presence of my husband, the neighbours and their gossip. I miss the sound of my alleys and the sun falling through the backyard,' said Kulwant.

'Interestingly, I don't miss my home at all. I missed my village when I moved to Delhi. If I close my eyes the image that I miss is that of my village, it's not that of the house in Delhi, even though the latter has been my home for many years now,' said Sitam.

'You know the Biharis say this the best,' Sitam continued. 'A Delhi University friend from Bihar would say, that in the vernacular, Biharis use two distinct words for home and they don't mean the same thing – they would say *ghar* and *dera*; ghar is home, which is always the village, ancestral home and *dera* is something that they currently lived in, irrespective of how long they have been living there. So, you see, despite a decade in Delhi, it is my *dera* – but my village near Gangtok in Sikkim shall be my home forever.'

'Awesome,' said Sunil, for he knew exactly what Sitam was sharing.

'I agree,' said Razia.

'For me home is where memories are strewn in every corner, every crack, in every sapling and every nook – home is where serendipity is possible every moment because there are so many things and so many memories stacked in every possible place; one does not know what will spill out from where!

'I think in such a home it is magical to find something we were not even searching for, only to realise that it is exactly what we always wanted to find – to realise that in associations and memories, rather than in objects and possessions lies true joy of living.

'No wonder some places we roamed, some fruits we plucked and savouries we ate, some streets we frequented and some cities we live in always manage to evoke an ache for no reason at all.'

Kulwant commented, 'Home is where serendipity is possible. I have rummaged shelves for a book and found a handwritten note instead. I have searched for a file and found a book with a notation instead. Serendipity comes with many faces – and all its faces are joyous. A very distant past is mostly rosier in hindsight, even when it was not as rosy then. The sepia toned dog-eared photograph always manages to bring a smile – through toothy faces, chubby cheeks, through bushy hairs, through ribonned pleats.

'When we change homes, we lose all of this. What we lose is more precious than what we gain. We lose life – irreparably and irreversibly. What can be more tragic than that!'

Razia picked up from there. 'Serendipity brings back a deluge. Details and events do not matter. Actually, the details are inconsequential. The associations are more powerful. *It makes us rewind – and in rewinding we relive*. It is the only way to make us believe that we reversed the forward march of life. The illusion of it is the only solace, which gives fuel to deal with the next moment – a hope that the next moment is not permanently lost and that I shall meet this moment many years later in some corner and hear it say – 'I know you.'

'Razia madam,' you are amazing,' said Sunil.

'But why did you ask this question Sunil – if we miss home?' asked Razia.

'You see, I told you all that I have a younger brother. The other day when lakhs of people in Delhi were lining to return home because Delhi was no longer safe as COVID spread, one amongst them who walked hundreds of miles right until Agra was my younger brother.

'I don't know why he did it, I don't know where he was returning to, because there is no one in the village anymore that he can go back to and he won't come to me. So, I wonder when his best bet was to remain in Delhi why did he choose to go out, and more importantly to where?'

'We don't know what true home is, Mr Paswan,' said Razia.

'Each one is in search for a place where he feels like he belongs – maybe he is in search of that. That would be his home,'

'And if he does not find it, then?' asked Sunil.

'Well, then he keeps walking,' said Razia.

11. James, but not a Bond!

Each one of the inmates of Hotel Landmark was dealing with being away from their families in a different way. No one plans for such long periods of distance from loved ones.

Consequences of choices made out of free will are easier to accept and deal with – however deeply anguishing they might be. *Consequences of circumstances thrust upon you are a burden on the soul – they demand a scapegoat if not an explanation.*

We express joys in similar ways. It is grief that is experienced in unique ways and is dealt with in even more unique ways.

Sitam was rediscovering solitude and even if he may not admit it, he was enjoying it. He had lived alone and away from family for more than a decade during his student days. There was almost a decade between the time he left his village and the time he got married. During this time, from being in a small home where a human being would be spilling over from every nook and corner of his house to living in a 3BHK where only the three of them were living, he had a full decade to enjoy solitude and freedom.

Staying alone spoils you. There is no noise. Silence is a companion. For the pensive, silence is priceless. You yearn for it – for every conversation with human beings is nothing short of violence.

Those who say that they like the company of others are liars. No human being in her senses likes the company of others more than they like their own company – and those who claim that they do, are either juveniles or have not yet experienced the sheer bliss of talking to that little bird in your head. Extroverts will take time to grow up.

Sitam had enjoyed this bliss for a decade when he got married and his life crashed after that. The idea that someone else would also stay with him, use his bathroom and sleep on the same bed and will ask questions at extraordinarily inopportune moments was a shock that he took months to deal with. He soon realised that this aspect of marriage took the greatest toll on him and this was also something no one was willing to empathise with him on. Most thought that he was insane even complaining about this.

Sitam realised that there is no greater violence against another human being than being forced to make small talk when all that person wants is silence. Most marriages are pretty violent by this yardstick.

So Sitam was rediscovering the joys of solitude. He would not care to admit it to his wife and children and most of all to himself, but he was actually enjoying being with himself after so many years.

It was not rediscovery but discovery for Kulwant. She had never stayed alone in her whole life. She did not know solitude. She had always believed that it is with people and family that the truest joys of life are discovered. She had detested the few times that she had been alone. She would call someone or the other to stay with her to avoid being alone.

Being alone was her single largest fear. The idea that the whole day there would be no one to share the small bits that had happened through the day was depressing. She had to share. It would be her parents on the phone or a very uninterested husband who would come home tired after the long day from work or even the neighbours – she needed people to hear her thoughts. 'After all is that not what family and friends are for?' she would often say to herself.

This lockdown was clearly the most difficult for her. Maybe she was too old to change her ways but for her, the first few days were worse than death in the family. She would talk to her husband and her parents and cry for hours.

Over the last few days she was starting to think differently. She was beginning to come to the conclusion that relationships survive because we get used to each other's presence and not because there is an eternal romantic glue that binds the two together. If you stay even with a stranger for long enough a familiarity will develop – and for the want of a better word, it's called love. People stay in marriages because the hassles of going through the painful process of building that familiarity all over again is too much to bear.

She was beginning to talk to herself. She was beginning to reminisce old incidents, the fights of childhood, the joys of school, friends who had studied with her and moved on, small incidents, games she played, the dolls she collected, the crazy period of her youthful love affair with the Muslim boy, the ruckus it created and so much more. Solitude has great power. It allows us to see the small moments buried deep beneath the dust of time. These moments are a balm for the bruised soul.

Kulwant may not still like the lockdown but it was clear she was the one benefitting from it the most.

Manoj was dealing with something unusual for him. He was for the first time, with a group of people who were not interested in how much he knew or how capable he was, or not even interested in how much he had achieved or could achieve. They cared a damn.

He did not know how to interact with people who were like that – who did not need anything from him, with whom there was no need to play one-upmanship, who need not be won over.

In fact, in the first few days, every time he tried to impress others with his views and knowledge, he was rebuffed with equal intensity. This was new wicket for him, and he realised he did not know how to play this.

How does one forge a conversation without superiority of knowledge; how does one build a relationship only on the basis of your being – bereft of every label that you have so far used to create your identity? So far Manoj was the sum of his education, the books he had read and his intelligence – he was nothing without them. Funnily, everyone in Hotel Landmark refused to acknowledge all of the above. They only wanted Manoj, the person, and that was a tall demand for Manoj, for even he did not know what Manoj was without these labels.

The solitude was helping him realise the futility of these labels. He had thought these labels helped him become a better person and build stronger relationships – but that was not how it was turning out.

Perhaps it is the curse of people who spend an enormous amount of their waking time at offices, that they confuse the reality of workplace as the reality of life. They use the norms of relationship building at workplace at home or with friends also, mistakenly believing that those norms will work. They miserably fail – and they realise it often too late. Those who are very capable, very educated and very successful are the most susceptible to this folly.

He had read somewhere that those who are very successful at work, die early after retirement and if they survive, they are a huge pain in everyone's ass. Thirty to forty years of workplace experience renders them unfit to live with human beings who are not bound to them by work relationships. Actually, dying is an easy escape for them and a big relief for the people around them.

Manoj was getting to see himself in a very new light and he was not liking what he was seeing.

All of them woke up to mostly gloomy news and only one potentially bright piece of news, but it was doubtful anyone registered the latter.

The number of dead in India because of the COVID infection rose to 70 with more than 2400 testing positive. The number worldwide had crossed a million. Country after country, state after state were discovering new hot spots and taking desperate measures. There was news of some idiots throwing stones at the health workers who had come to test suspected cases and some other news of suspected patients being violent with doctors and nurses.

Even in a crisis like this human stupidity can shine through. *Goodness and stupidity are both just a trigger away.*

There are many mysteries in life that are difficult to explain and one of the most profound of them is – Why do good people do bad things, and why do bad people do good things?

Hidden amidst this gloom was a small piece of bright news – that 132 of the COVID patients had been cured and returned to their homes safely, but no one noticed it.

Dinner that night in Hotel Landmark was spent playing cardboard games and singing songs while playing *antakshari*. Most were horrible singers but hardly anyone noticed.

When they got tired of singing songs, they started to ask each other questions about their families and their childhood and interesting tit bits. It had taken them 10 days in captivity to be seriously interested in each other's stories.

They asked how they were as children, of the naughtiest things they had done at school, a coming of age story, something they had done as a youngster without their parents knowing, the first time they smoked or drank alcohol. They were like young boys and girls that night.

Everyone poured their heart out and spoke more freely than they thought they could. It is difficult to share about the devil in you with friends and family because you run the risk of being judged but it can be done with strangers, for not only will they not judge you, but even if they do, you do not have to face them thereafter.

Strangers make the best psychiatrists. When you meet a stranger, you should share your darkest desires – of wanting to kill someone close, of your desire to make love to someone you should not be thinking of that way and many more crazy things.

'Let's tell each other one instance where you were overjoyed to meet a stranger,' suggested Kulwant. 'A positive story which overwhelmed you and reinforced your belief in the goodness of people.'

'I think we need our quota of positivity desperately,' said Sitam. 'Negative stories are sticky. Let's change the game,'

'That is a great idea,' chipped in Razia. 'Let's do one per day – we have 10 days more to go and we are only four'

'Five,' corrected Sunil Paswan, with a smile.

'Ok ok. Who goes first?' asked Razia.

'I will go first,' – said Manoj.

'Shoot,' – said everyone in unison.

'The hero of my story is James,' began Manoj, in a dramatic tone.

'Bond?' asked everyone like school kids waiting to pull the leg of the first performer.

'Nah – better than the Bond,' replied an even more dramatic Manoj.

'I got talking to my Uber driver named James on an early morning drive. I do that often. Each time there is a different story but this one turned out to be the most enjoyable and inspiring.

'The difference between him and others whom I had met till then was clear right from his answer to my first question. He told me he had four cabs; this one he drove and the other three have been rented to other drivers. Soon he switched to conversing in English, as if he had sensed that I had made the error of stereotyping him.

'He told me that he was from Lucknow, had done his MBA and had worked in a few banks as a frontline seller of banking products, growing up to become a territory manager – and soon he had a house and a flourishing business of solar panels.

'However, a business deal gone sour caused the collapse of his business with huge bank overruns. Something radical had to be done to pay off the bank. So, with a heavy heart he sold the house and paid the banks completely because he did not want his CIBIL ratings to suffer at any cost. Here was someone who in his darkest hour was more worried about his credit credibility!

'He and his wife decided to send their son back to Lucknow so that both of them could focus on rebuilding their lives. He told me that he had not left his home to be a loser and that at all costs he had to keep moving forward.

'I asked him what his plans were. I was frankly not prepared for the answer I got. James replied 'I plan to repay the loan on all my taxis and become debt free. Then I want to open an NGO. Do you know that many NGOs are working to clean the Ganga in Kanpur? I want to do something around education. You see, when I worked for myself things did not work quite well, let me now try doing something for others – who knows what the outcome will be. '*Apne liye kaam kiya to nuksaan hua, doosron ke liye kar ke dekhte hain*'

'I asked him if he had any regrets. He replied 'Nothing actually. Even when I sold the house, I told myself, perhaps that is why the house was built – to bail us out during this crisis. The only thing that pains me is that I had to send my son away from me to tide over this. I miss him.'

'He asked me for my card so that he could call me when he opened his NGO.

'James was a better Bond than all those I had seen so far,' – ended Manoj.

There was a stunning silence at the end and the only thing more surprising and pleasant about this story was the fact that it was Manoj who shared this.

12. Daring in Dimples

What the four strangers who were now warming up to each other in Hotel Landmark in Mumbai did not realise, was that the lockdown, which was bringing so much change in the way they looked at themselves and others around them, was on the other hand bringing the rest of the world to a standstill in ways no one had ever imagined.

Every generation has stories about a few events in their lifetime that are heirloom stories, repeated *ad infinitum* to the level that they become *ad nauseum.*

Old enough grandparents had stories of the freedom struggle, the stories of the birth of the nation, the story of ideals and sacrifices.

The next generation talked about the various wars India fought with Pakistan and the Emergency, the long queues and the atmosphere of scarcity, and finally the stories of their own parsimoniousness. Both these generations talk about their times with sepia-coloured hues and a sense of righteousness, as if those stories made them morally taller than the next generation.

One had to give it to them that they indeed understood struggle, that they indeed had to fight it out to survive and what they created was in the face of strong limitations. They deserved to tell those stories.

The generations thereafter have been singularly unlucky in one big way – they have had no romantic stories of struggle to share. They got luckier in terms of facilities, opportunities, resources, and economic prosperity, but became paupers in terms of their right to brag about making it big amidst remarkable constraints. They achieved a lot and became successful surely but did so because of rather favourable circumstances; the generations before that did so despite them.

There is no doubt that every few years some calamity or the other visited some part of the country – in the form of riots, floods, epidemics and terrorist attacks. However, all of them were localised at most. Most people could watch the tumult in the cosy comforts of their drawing rooms, smug in the satisfaction that the problem belonged to someone else. There was a belief that this wouldn't reach their doorsteps and despite their posturing of shock, it was clear on their faces that they were secure in their hides.

COVID and this scare was different – this was perhaps the first time most living people in the country were experiencing a scare as large, as unknown and as widespread as this. The enemy this time certainly was at their gates.

Cities had come to a standstill. Fear was rampant. Every day some new part of the country and the world came to know that their smugness was ill-informed. There were still ten more days of the lockdown to go and no one was sure any longer if by the end of those ten days the menace would not reach their doorsteps.

A large part of our resolve to fight an adversary is the hope of the light at the end of the tunnel. If you do not see it, the resolve itself becomes feeble. *Human resolve to remain in a fight depends on whether they see a possibility of victory to begin with.*

The four guests of Hotel Landmark found in the news that yet another 500 people had tested COVID positive in the country the previous day, taking the total beyond 3000. The numbers were multiplying at a rate faster than the first few days and even the greatest optimist was rethinking. The deaths across the world were not abating.

They also found that many doctors and healthcare professionals were also succumbing to the virus, and that a leading virologist in South Africa, someone of Indian descent also died owing to COVID complications.

The country was halfway through the most unprecedented lockdown that they had ever seen and at that halfway mark, there was absolutely nothing that gave hope for things becoming better. Everyone was relying on prayers.

The four guests also read some interesting stories on social media. There was news from across the country that air pollution levels had fallen to unprecedented levels. The air everyone was breathing was fresher, crisper and cleaner. Residents of Jalandhar in Punjab woke up to see the snow-capped Dhauladhar ranges in Himachal Pradesh, a good 213 kilometres away – it was a sight only the previous generation had enjoyed. In Haridwar and many other places people found deer walking on roads, peacocks playing in the locality, sparrows remerging in cities and the chirping of birds had become common. *Earth had started to breathe again – even when the patients of COVID were on ventilators.*

‘Shall we continue with the stories?’ asked Razia, excited as a school kid. There was something about the storytelling that she had taken a liking to. Manoj had set a great benchmark.

‘Who will go today?’ asked Kulwant.

‘Maybe I will give it a shot,’ said Sitam.

‘Remember the condition guys – it has to be positive, inspirational and joyous. It must make us feel happy and gay,’ reminded Razia.

‘Happy, sure; gay you better not,’ winked Manoj.

‘PJ,’ said Razia. Their banter was becoming warmer by the day.

‘Will try,’ reassured Sitam.

‘So, this was when I was on a flight once. It would be a lie if I claimed that I did not notice the dimples on the fellow passenger as I took my seat. As everyone got busy, I saw that she was struggling to plug her mobile in the charging point between the seats and asked for help. I tried to help but could not. There was something wrong with the plug point itself. We called the air hostess and struggled together, finally realising that it could not be done – the faulty plug point had however managed to break the ice.’

‘As is the wont of two travellers, both of us got talking. Travel companionship is a strange phenomenon – no one can predict if and to what extent it will blossom. It can range from the meaningless to the profound.

‘Sometimes you don’t strike a conversation as you want to be left alone, to brood or to reflect. Sometimes the vibes are not good and at other times when the vibes are good, sheer hesitation nips in infancy, what could have been a great possibility. I wondered how this one would be. Thankfully the plug point came to the rescue.

'It took an hour or so to wrap up the basic information exchange – of who we were, our destinations, and other such banalities, which form the basic foundation of what can be termed as the sizing-each-other-up stage between strangers. The result of this exchange decides if there is anything whatsoever in common, if there is any chemistry or vibes, that will serve as the foundation of a conversation. I call this the anatomy of conversation between strangers. The half-life of such conversations and relationships usually is the duration of the flight.

'I had Leo Tolstoy's Anna Karenina in my hands and she asked me what the book was about. I told her my impressions of the book – that it was about love, relationships, class and the futility of high society pretentions. Something changed in her eyes as I spoke – I don't know which part had that impact. I described Anna, the lead protagonist of the novel to her – that she was fiery and beautiful, courageous and iconoclast, fragile and strong, all at the same time. She smiled and said Anna sounded like her. I asked her to explain.

'She told her story like grannies do – to the point, with a certain detachment that only wisdom has the capability to achieve. She shared that she fell in love at an early age and decided to marry much against the wishes of the family. Youth has a mind of its own. Soon the dream sequence turned into a nightmare as the scourge of domestic violence and mental harassment raised its head. It was difficult to deal with the twin trauma of the situation – of the agony of the circumstance at hand and of the corroding pain that it was brought upon her by the error of her own judgement.

'I could imagine the helplessness of a young person tormented by the burden of a choice gone horribly wrong; of her hesitation in seeking help from family who might have said that one thing that a person in trouble wants to hear the least – I told you so! So, one day she gathered courage, called in the cops, broke free, reached out to her family and put an end to this misery.

'A few years later love came calling again when a colleague evinced interest in her. After seeking parental consent, she agreed. I asked her if it was difficult to give love another chance. She said it was not very difficult, particularly after a very encouraging discussion with her father, who assured her that she should not stop making choices just because one choice had gone wrong, that she must not lose faith in her instinct to search for happiness despite knowing that at the end of the day it's a roll of dice. *Just because it's a roll of dice does not mean we don't play the game.*

'In the manner in which she was recounting the story I saw neither regret, nor pain, neither anguish nor grief – just a recollection of events as they had occurred. Her nonchalance was refreshing in times when it is fashionable to portray ourselves as victims.

'As the plane taxied on the runway a few hours later we bid goodbye to each other like strangers do at the end of the journey. The story remained with me though – of courage, of optimism, of dusting off the fall and getting up again to give life another chance. As she smiled with the goodbye, the last thing I remember seeing were the dimples – dimples that had dared.'

As Sitam finished the story there was a smile on everyone's face.

It was Manoj who said the last word that day – 'Ahm, did you take her phone number?'

13. Love Dies

Each one of them thought about the storytelling sessions as they went to sleep – of course, in different ways.

Manoj was surprised that he could indulge in such a juvenile way of spending time. His fundamental nature was challenged when an activity was done without a clear purpose and benefit. His obsession with time never allowed him such luxuries. He was someone who even calendarized the intimate time with spouse and children! He had to always be clear about why he was doing something and an even acuter clarity of the gains emerging out of doing it. So, it surprised him that he was doing storytelling for the soft and fuzzy reason of remaining positive.

Kulwant was surprised because each of the stories was touching her in ways she was not used to. There was something long-forgotten that was coming to the surface, reminding her of an old hurt, an old anguish, as if a buried volcano was finding a way out. The James story reminded her how she had moved on from one stage of life to another without giving a thought to herself and her needs, while the girl with the dimple story reminded her of what she was not – she wished she had the courage to move on from things, people and circumstances, when they were not working out for her.

Sitam was surprised because he never knew he had the ability to tell a story. He had taken pride in his being a matter of fact person – someone whose ability to deal with adversity emerged from a deep-seated confidence. He had always mocked those who read too many self-help books or took recourse to motivational seminars. He had believed that such people were weak and delusional. They were searching outside for what should be inside. He also believed it was the privileged ones who needed such outside help – people like him who grew up through tough circumstances have a fountain of confidence and courage deep inside them.

After the two stories he was wondering if he had been unfair to such people – there was nothing wrong in people finding their own sources of courage and calm. Who was he to judge them? If a straw saves a drowning person, that straw is worth a thousand logs!

Razia was a sucker for such stories. She always had been. Her belief in the fundamental goodness of men and women was only getting stronger. Her surprise after two stories had been that both these stories came from people she had least expected them to come from – Manoj and Sitam.

She was learning a hard truth – everyone has stories. It takes a lockdown to open up!

Sunil Paswan was itching to tell his own story; for him there was nothing more positive and inspirational than his own story. He thought to himself that Life made sense only in retrospect. While life is happening, the joys appear heady and unreal, while grief is like undergoing an operation without anaesthesia. One is so engrossed in dealing with the joys and grief, that making sense of it is the last thing on our mind. He realised that the past often looks hazy and details are often lost. The details one remembers are only those that we have told and retold many times as a raconteur. Actually, the version that we tell ourselves is often a version which we have carried with us while the truth had drifted away.

There are two possible drifts – either we overplay struggles to glorify them or underplay them because we feel blessed to have overcome them. *Struggles are struggles only when we are going through them – when it all ends, they are mere memories.*

We realise that forgetfulness is actually our ally. One wonders if it is actually a good thing or not – for forgetfulness helps in dealing with the tribulations that leave a scar, but it also makes us forget what gave us profound joy.

Sunil was thankful that he had a vague memory, most details for him were often lost. He realised that this had helped him immensely to overcome all that pain and anguish of his early life. Forgetfulness provides us the capability to move ahead.

The second thing he realised was that our stories are always flattering to us. We are always the heroes and heroines of our stories. It is difficult to look back at our lives and conclude that we have been villains of our lives, even though it may actually be true.

The third thing that he realised was how blessed he was. His story, despite its hiccups, had turned out quite well. He was reminded of a recent movie dialogue and smiled to himself – *'picture abhi baaki hai mere dost'*.

It was not lost upon all the inmates of Hotel Landmark that the second half of the 21-day lockdown had begun. Human beings calculate the gradient of their challenge in very strange ways. The second half of a journey appears shorter than the first part. Crossing the mid-way of a challenge often gives a sudden surge to our resolve to see it through.

The second half may be more frustrating because the duration would appear longer, but the first half is always more demanding on our resolve.

The lockdown was throwing up some very crazy responses. It was reported that some people in Tamil Nadu drank after-shave because alcohol was in short supply. On the other hand people were finding ingenious ways of keeping themselves engaged and fit. Some ran a few kilometres within the confines of their homes and yet others were running marathons on their balconies. In fact, balconies had become the theatre of liberation in the times of lockdown. Thieves had become ingenious too. They were stealing what had suddenly become more precious. Alcohol bottles from wine shops and even government custody were being stolen.

Matters of temporal often met matters of spirituality. Apparently, the police had arrested a baba somewhere in the state of Uttar Pradesh, who was claiming a cure for COVID and had been appropriately named – *corona wale baba*. It was still to be seen if he had found a cure from the treatment he would have been meted out by the famous UP police. The rumour has it that they can cure even the incurable, some say they can cure what is not yet a disease.

In one part of the country an outfit had its scientific temperament in full display when they worshipped cow urine, cow dung treatment and clicked pictures of attendees sipping cow urine as their protection against the outbreak of COVID. Stupidity is not the reserve of one country. It is an international virtue. There was a South African politician who had called the Coronavirus scare 'God's punishment to the West'. It was not yet known if the President of the US took that personally, but he did come out with a statement the very same day, 'wearing masks is recommended but I will not wear one'. It clearly seems that there is some truth in the pronouncement of the South African – with intelligence such as the one demonstrated by the President, they indeed deserved God's fury. However, what really takes the cake is the Malaysian government's advisory for women. They suggested that under such dire circumstances women must wear make-up at all times, should not nag their husbands and speak in a soothing voice like cartoon characters. Stupidity is an international infection!

There was good news too. There were hundreds of news items where people were rising above the subject of their own safety and wellbeing and serving the poor, the needy and the sick. The most evolved of human instinct, of goodness, of service, of sharing and care, of sacrifice and of going beyond the call of duty was on full display. The world still had hope.

At the same time the worst in human beings was also at display. Villages, neighbourhoods and localities were closing themselves to the outside world, restricting the traffic of outsiders and strangers. They were not doing it as a precaution – they were doing it so that they could exclude outsiders. The instinct was to build a cocoon around themselves and consider everyone outside that cocoon as dangers to be avoided.

A crisis brings out the best and the worst in us!

At lunch the hot topic of discussion was what to do with the call by the Prime Minister to switch off lights and light a *diya* or a candle. The merits, real and imagined were outlined with passion – of course Manoj was leading the praise. Not surprisingly, the charge against the action was led by Sitam – calling it meaningless, hollow and a cheap stunt when what the country needed was real action.

The trouble with debates about politics is that you take a stand first and then you defend it. During the course of the debate even if you discovered that there are anomalies, imperfections and flaws in your political ideology, icons, heroes and the political stance itself, there is no scope for retreat. Admitting those flaws is considered as conceding political defeat; in matters of the political, that is hara-kiri.

We get entrapped deeper and deeper in our own stances. Logic and objectivity be damned. That is exactly what plays out in almost all political debates, they are nothing less than parlour games. Everyone plays to spend time. The outcome is inconsequential.

We arrive at the conclusions first and fit the proof later, that is if, we are conscientious enough.

Kulwant wanted to break the *tu tu mai mai* between Sitam and Manoj and suddenly interjected – 'do you know what someone wise replied when he was asked if he was right wing or left wing?'

Everyone waited because everyone knew that it was not a question asked to be answered.

'He replied that – *'I am for the whole bird'*. A one-winged bird didn't ever get off the ground.'

Both Sitam and Manoj got the hint and gradually allowed the meaningless debate to settle.

It was Razia who came up with a brilliant idea for the evening.

'Let's do a candlelight dinner!'

'I mean why only for nine minutes. Let's celebrate our friendship over a candlelight dinner for the whole evening – let it mean something for us at least.'

Everyone concurred and looked at Sunil Paswan hopefully, a look that he just could not understand.

'Why are you all looking at me like that?' he asked still puzzled.

It was Razia who asked the question everyone had in their minds.

'Do you have enough candles?'

When they came down for dinner, the place had acquired a new look altogether. Lights were dim and the dining area was all candle-lit. PM Modi's idea of candle and *diya* lighting may have been intended as a symbolism but here the candle-lit setting was serving a very different purpose.

Somehow, they were dressed for the occasion. They had decided that they would make an occasion out of that evening. *We can either make an occasion out of nothing or make nothing out of occasions.*

There are parties one goes to and feels lonely. The burden of keeping a pretence of amicability is far heavier than any soul can imagine. However, some parties bring a spring to the soul. In a very strange way, this evening was doing the same for each one of them. Each one of them was surprised at their excitement for a different reason.

Perhaps it was a dozen days in captivity or maybe it was the yellow flickering light of the candles, the topics that were discussed amongst them were all warm and mushy. It is funny how just a change of settings can change what kind of conversations will happen amongst people. Soft music here, a little dimming light there, a bit of fragrance to top things up is almost certain to put people in the mood to talk subjects of the soul.

'What do you think of love?' Razia was the first to throw the gauntlet.

'It is a worthwhile idea,' commented the ever-cynic Manoj. '*People are not as much in love as much as they are in love with the idea of love.*'

'You see, what you call love is more about compatibility and shared interests. Throw in a bout of chemistry, a bit of sexual tension and lo behold we have a concoction called love.'

'You make it sound like it's cooked in the chemistry laboratory,' commented Razia.

'Not too far my friend – not too far. It is indeed a *chemical locha,*' pontificated Manoj.

Sitam began – 'Difficult to define, difficult to talk about

it – but you know it when you have it. It's like what someone said about pornography – that one cannot define it, but one would know it when one sees it.'

'But everyone should fall in love for sure. A life is not worth living if one has not gone through its poetic highs and its ridiculous lows. When one is going through the stupidities that love makes you do, they appear meaningful and cute – a few years later you look back upon it and almost crack open in embarrassment that it was you who did all that. Yet, it is better to do it once rather than not do it all. *It is those stories about love that last you a lifetime, long after love has died.'*

'You mean love is nothing but stories of a brief period that you remember for a long time?' asked Manoj.

'Bang on!' said Sitam. 'Love, or at least the madness of love, does not last forever, but those stories are told and retold a million times. In those retellings the fires of love get an extension – otherwise the embers would extinguish sooner than you think.'

'Love is responsibilities *sirjee,*' commented the wise Mr Sunil Paswan, now a permanent presence. 'It's about keeping the fires of the kitchen burning, bringing food and security home. It's about knowing all that is not even being spoken. Silence tests love the most.'

'Well said Sunil,' praised Kulwant. 'But does love die?' she dropped a bombshell. No one answered. Noticing the silence, Kulwant herself started to dwell deeper.

'There is no greater torment in life than to keep the pretence of love alive. In most relationships love dies and all of us at some time or the other wake up to find love dead.

We discover what we thought as love was only its corpse.

'Most relationships are not prepared for this stage but there is no escape from confronting this stage. It is as natural and normal as the beginning of twilight after the bright day. Yet no one is prepared for it.

'People mistake fights for the death of a relationship – actually it's the absence of anything common left to talk about that is the real end of relationships. Fights mean there is some trace of love still left.

'All love dies,' ended Kulwant.

Stunned silence on the table greeted that.

'I need a refill,' said Sitam. 'So, do I,' added Razia and Manoj.

'Ek hamara bhi,' asked Sunil, hesitantly.

'I will also have one,' said Kulwant.

At that point everyone knew that the evening was already a success. No one remembered to do it, but they should have done it – thank Prime Minister Modi.

14. Resplendence in Impurities

The previous evening's bonhomie was lingering on everyone's mind as they woke up – drunk and drowsy. Most of all Kulwant. She was not the same person she had been the previous day. There were many firsts for her.

Kulwant had a drink for the first time. She had it with strangers. She had it when she was away from family. She did not know why she had it, but not only did she have it, she actually enjoyed having it.

She giggled like she had not giggled in a long time. She joked and laughed and back slapped – although she may not remember whose back. She sang songs, first the melodious ones and then the naughty ones. She vaguely remembered singing and dancing on the popular drunken number of her times – *'Jai Jai Shiv Shankar/Kanata lage na kankar'*. What she was not able to digest was that she was standing on the table when she was singing it! She had notions of propriety and manners that had governed her so far, shaped by the patriarchal Punjabi society. All her life she was able to or not able to do things based on what was considered ok according to the norms of her family and that society. Every time she had taken a decision, whether she liked it or not, she would think about the potential reactions of everyone around her – parents, husband, children, neighbours and friends. In a lot of ways, none of her decisions really were hers. Over time this approval seeking had become a part of her soul.

She had felt liberated yesterday. She felt liberated from each and every approval she had ever sought. She felt free of all the bondages that she had carried with her. She finally did something that did not involve seeking anyone's approval – in words or in essence. Some approvals are not really required but we are just not free enough. The dark abyss of the human heart is like an elephant who does not forget his chains long after they are gone. Sometimes there are no chains – it's just that we are not free. *No amount of freedom can free a soul which is convinced of its chains.*

However, the one liberation that she was particularly proud of that morning was from a story that she had told herself over and over again in the recent times – that she is too old to do this or that. She had broken free of that chain and at her stage in life, it was most important to her. There was a reason for that. She knew that all the other chains were tied at some stage or the other by people in her life who had some power over her; this was the only chain she had tied around her by herself. She had no one else to blame for it. Hence it was her greatest joy to break it and say – to hell with my age! After all isn't age just a number?

Most sixty-year-olds would tell you that the bloody number does not do justice to what they feel about themselves.

The 20s are times when one wants to do stuff and can actually do it although one may not be able to afford it always.

The 30s are when one can afford it, can do it as well and often end up doing it, although sometimes not knowing why.

At 40 one can certainly afford it, know why they should do it, but these are times when life holds you under its clutches. Responsibilities do not allow you to breathe and enjoy what you can finally afford and do.

At 50, one knows that the best of years are behind us, when for the first time one realises that the body is not able to do what the mind and the heart believes can be done easily. One becomes acutely aware of this dissonance between the heart and the body. For example, climbing 10 flights of stairs makes you feel that the heart is trying to jump out of its place; or sometimes wearing the latest fashion and seeing others' heart actually jump ouf of its place.

At 60, the dominant thought is – 'Shit – it's over'. A proverb says it so well – "If only youth knew and age could".

Kulwant had heard many praising her, 'You have aged gracefully,' and she had hated it. How much she had wanted to say, 'but who wants to age?' It is such a scary feeling to know that life as we know it is gone.

The desires give more ache and grief than a reason to live. You have no grand purpose to wake up to the next morning and look forward to the day unfolding. There is nothing that kills a soul more than the fact that it has nothing to look forward to the next morning.

Yesterday, Kulwant broke those chains and on the 13th day of the lockdown, woke up a liberated woman. She was finally free.

∞

The country had a lot to deal with on the 13th day of the lockdown. Social media was ablaze by the Prime Minister's previous night's call to light *diyas* and candles. One thing about social media is very clear – there is nothing social about it.

Millions showed support to whatever the lighting of *diyas* was meant to signify – solidarity, shared purpose, common enemy or pure symbolism of all being in it together. They came out in hordes and did what was required. They flashed lights, lit candles, chanted 'Go Corona Go' and 'Bharat Mata ki Jai'. In 9 minutes, the country went back to their bedrooms and got on with their lives.

Then there were those who called it dramatics and an empty ploy of distraction. The cynics who could not think of anything better to do, spent time criticising those who were trying to do something – even symbolism has power. *Religions, nations, organisations, families and relationships – all will crumble within a day if not for the steroid of symbolism.*

Social media became the subject of a small debate at the lunch table – as usual it was difficult to keep politics and social media separate from each other, till Sunil Pawan showed to them that the previous day had liberated him too.

'Have you looked at Twitter today – I think people have gone mad. Here is a PM who is trying to bring the people together and there are lakhs who are criticising him. I mean is this the time to stand with him or criticise him?' fumed Manoj.

'Spoken like a true *bhakt,*' commented Sitam.

'You must be a *sickular* then – or a *libtard,*' retorted Manoj immediately.

'Ah! So, you know these words,' sarcasm at its best by Sitam.

'Well, I know the words and I know those people too,' pure menace by Manoj.

'At least the PM will know what his army of IT cell trolls do to the rest,' came the next salvo by Sitam.

'Not everyone who disagrees with your agenda is a troll,' philosophised Manoj.

'Precisely the point – if only the IT cell trolls understand that,' jibed Sitam.

Score 1-0. Game continued.

'What is wrong in calling out lies that have been pedalled for more than half a century?' asked Manoj.

'Wrong is the manner in which these guys do it,' said Sitam.

'What is their manner?' not an innocent one, but a question, nonetheless.

'A troll hides behind a mob. He is like the faceless member of the herd who seeks strength in his anonymity and protection in his being unknown. He is the neighbourhood bully who lurks around the corner with a group of lumpen elements. I also suspect he is psychologically deeply disturbed and must have had a history of attention deficiency. He is battling his insignificant past and most likely even more insignificant future – someone who is busy trolling is unlikely to achieve anything meaningful anytime soon, particularly by attacking those who are genuinely significant enough to have attracted trolls.'

'And such behaviour is only in one kind of trolls – as you call them?' asked Manoj; a sensible question.

'That is true. This behaviour is found in all kinds of trolls – irrespective of whether they are *bhakts* or *libtartds* as you put it,' said Sitam with a wry smile.

'A troll expresses without processing. A troll rarely cross-checks facts and verifies truthfulness. Actually, he has nothing to do with truth – he draws fun out of the attack. The grounds of the attack be damned.'

Razia jumped, in 'I have also noticed another peculiarity about trolls — A troll has an opinion on anything and everything. A successful troll has something to say even when he has no clue on the subject at hand. My sense is that he actually knows nothing about anything at all because anyone who has any credible knowledge about anything would not do something as silly as offering unsolicited advice or comments. *Restraint – as a word, ability and attitude is unknown to a troll.'*

She continued with a smile on her face this time 'A troll is touchy and hence aggressive. He is touchy about his views and his position in general. Maybe he suffers from low self-esteem and was most likely thrashed by his teachers and parents. As a troll this is payback time for him. He will criticise anyone for anything. *Most of his hurt is imaginary but his digital anger is real.'*

This back and forth continued till they had nothing else to say. The debate of pros and cons on the PM remained unresolved and so did the subject of *bhakts* and *sickulars*. Perhaps in their hearts they knew that these were unreal debates.

Thereafter, they talked about things happening around the world. They talked about a group of Kolkata police singing songs below a residential apartment, in other places the police donning artistic corona shaped attire and finding creative ways of asking people to stay at home, at one place even doing *aarti* of those who had the temerity to venture out.

Meanwhile, they also read that the total number of fatalities in India had crossed 100, the total number of infected crossed 4000, the infection had reached 257 out of 640 districts within 15 days – a number which was only 62 districts a fortnight ago. The scourge was already present in almost half the country. The number of dead the previous day was yet again more than 500, that was the third day a row.

A similar number for the world was a shade higher than 60,000 dead and more than 11 lakh tested positive.

The mood of the world and the nation despite its valiant efforts was just not turning positive. News was only about lakhs of job losses and job cuts that were likely to happen. The stock markets had tumbled by more than a third and a large number of people had seen a level of wealth erosion that they had only heard about in textbooks. This time it was real and this time it was *their* wealth.

Companies were threatening to close. Everyone was afraid – some of the virus, and others of what was still to come. *A world without resources is easy to fix – a world without hope is dead much before anything could be done.*

Families in the lockdown were creating funny memes and if one were to preserve all the memes created during this lockdown and they were to be opened a few decades later by our children – they would be shocked at the depressing quality of taste, humour and creativity. Thankfully that was going to happen in the future. In any case, we do find all that our past generation did mostly in poor taste and utterly bereft of sophistication. So, it should not be any different in this case, although it must be added that this time, they were genuinely atrocious.

It is funny how mass delusion works. Sometimes it robs you of hope when you have all the reasons to be hopeful. Sometimes, it makes you disregard danger even when all signs are indicating towards it. It was difficult to know which case it was on the 13th day of the lockdown.

If one were to see the way numbers were moving, it was clear we were hurtling down the precipice; if one were to go by the bonhomie amongst the inmates of Hotel Landmark, it was clear that a new world was being created – at least for all of them.

Our worlds are never out there. Our worlds are what is happening to us.

'Whose turn is it to tell a story?' Kulwant raised the subject at dinner.

'I will go for it,' said Razia. And she began...

'I was travelling by Kerala state transport bus, those rickety things that move Keralites from one part of the state to another, and the speed at which they are driven they would perhaps take off, if they got sufficiently long runways.' It was an interesting start, everyone thought.

'Since this was an overnight journey, the bus had to stop for passengers to have dinner. So, it did stop at one of those roadside places on highways that have a rhythm of their own – blaring music, rushed orders, hot food and garishly decorated walls – anything that will bring some energy to tired bodies. Dealing with night coach buses is generally difficult; in Kerala it is a nightmare.

'I saw an old man playing with multi-coloured stones on a table. Since he was from my bus only and I had no other vacant table, I asked him if I could join him at his table. He found the idea irritating but agreed – or at least he did not say no. I did not have too many choices, so I sat down.

'He kept playing with his stones, perhaps a dozen, of all shapes and all hues. His eyes twinkled as he picked up one of them, looked intently and then as if the stone had spoken to him, he would keep it back. He would repeat that with the next stone.

'Are you a collector?' I could not help asking.

'He did not reply. I was more intrigued than interested. I had heard of people interested in stamps and mugs and coins – but was seeing someone obsessed with such coloured stones for the first time. We find strange human beings interesting – normal is boring. It's only when strangeness becomes weird that our senses give us warnings. The old man was not giving me any weird vibes.

'The old man was giving me the vibes of someone who was interesting, someone who had a story to tell. So, I persisted and asked him if he would like to have some coffee. This time he looked up and nodded. This was coffee diplomacy at its best.

'As I sat down with two cups of coffee on the table, he looked at me more warmly this time. He shared that he was a retired geologist by profession and one of the things that he was always fascinated by was the colours in which the stones came. He talked about gemmology, which is the study of gems. He shared that there are many ways in which gems are classified; for instance as precious or semi-precious, and then he shared that of the many factors on which their relative appeal and price depends upon, colour is an important one.

'Then he waited for a short moment and added that this aspect of gemmology can teach human beings a thing or two. It was clear that I was going to have an interesting coffee at that table that night.

'He shared that the precious stones are diamonds, rubies, sapphires and emeralds, with all other gemstones being semi-precious. Sapphire and Ruby, two of the most popular gems are actually cousins – both are *corundums*; that is made up of aluminium oxide, but different in the nature of impurities. The impurity Chromium gives it a red hue and is called a *Ruby*, while an impurity of Iron or Titanium will give it a blue or green or pink or purple colour and it will then be called a *Sapphire*.

'Then he went on to talk about Beryl or chemically beryllium aluminium cyclosilicate, which is a large joint family. The same culprit Chromium there gives it a green colour and then it's called an *Emerald*, the impurity of Iron gives it a golden colour. He talked about it with many examples – that the gem lovers...have these impurities to thank, for what...would have been a Ruby, Sapphire or Emerald without its colour?

'*An impurity or an imperfection so to speak, is the reason for the value of the stone. Take away its imperfection and it's just a stone.*

'Human beings treat an imperfection in a very different way. It's something to be detested, hated, criticized, corrected, feed-backed. What appears as an imperfection Maybe something that *we* do not like, something that *we* are not comfortable accepting, or something that is unacceptable to *our* sensibilities and not something that Maybe fundamentally or universally unlikable or wrong or bad.

'Ultimately good and bad Maybe nothing more than what we as individuals are comfortable or not comfortable with. Our own sensibilities cannot and must not decide what is an imperfection in a human being, a right that we defend with passion for ourselves, but something that we may not be willing to lend to others with similar passion.

'Aggression, forthrightness, ambition, result orientation, candour and courage can be virtues with double edges. One man's food can be another man's poison, one man's freedom fighter Maybe another man's terrorist, and one man's imperfection may actually be another man's virtue. Who knows for better or for worse, how a person might look once you take away what to you appears as an imperfection? Take away the impurity of Chromium and a Ruby is just another stone. It would be wise before we judge in people what would be an impurity to our eyes, but if he were to get rid of it, he might also rid himself of his greatest strength, the one thing that might be his greatest ally in the fight against mediocrity. Not all imperfections need to be eradicated in human beings – mostly it's not possible, sometimes it's not desired.

'On that muggy night on that highway, that old man ended up teaching me that while dealing with human beings, the big question to ask is, can the impurities or imperfections be valued for what they are, or what they could be, rather than what it is not or what it cannot ever be? Ultimately that is the difference between a gemmologist and a stone collector.'

15. *Sab Maaya Hai*

'*Sab moh maya hai madam,*' began Sunil, in his element, combining the best of Bihar and Bombay.

'*Kya moh maya hai Sunil ji?*' asked Kulwant – two inmates who were closest to real life philosophers.

'All of this. Every time something big happens, people start talking about changing the way we live. They start talking about how friends and family are our real wealth and all this hoarding of material things and maddening race to acquire wealth is so meaningless. During riots, floods, calamities or when people see dear ones die, they talk about how utterly meaningless these things are – and then within a few days everyone goes back to living the same life with the same obsessions,' said Sunil.

'Life has a funny way of deflecting our attention from what is most important Mr Paswan. 'Life is cunning.'

'You call life cunning Kulwant ji?'

'Indeed, life is cunning – it misleads you to have misplaced priorities. Today everyone is talking about how little it takes to live, the entire cost is actually the standard of living we have got used to; yet these will be the very people who will go out and spend on things that they had declared to be unimportant only a few days back. It appears we suffer from mass schizophrenia – we live two lives, one that we propound and the one that we live. This dichotomy becomes pronounced during such calamities,' said Kulwant.

'People become temporary philosophers,' said Sunil with lips curled in sarcasm.

'Well said Sunilji,' commented Kulwant.

'...and you know what is the favourite phrase of such temporary philosophers?'

'What?'

'*Sab moh maya hai,*' mocked Sunil.

Kulwant laughed to no end, clearly agreeing.

When the bout of laughter ebbed, she asked 'So what all do you think is *moh maaya* Sunil?' Kulwant had figured out over the last two weeks that Sunil was far wiser than what he projected. He remained servile because all said and done, they were his guests. Even though they had included him in their lives here, he had never crossed the line that exists between the guest and a manager.

Kulwant knew that here was a man of limited means but someone who had seen enough life. His understanding of people, their behaviour, their circumstances and how these can constrain the human soul was far deeper than most.

'What do I think, madam?' asked Sunil, surprised that his opinion was being sought on such a deep subject.

'Yes, what do you think of what all is *moh maaya* in life?'

Sunil went silent for many moments and then he began – first slowly and then in a flow.

'I have figured out that time itself is *moh maaya*. There is nothing whatsoever that will change as the dates change. The sun will go about its job tomorrow morning just as diligently as it has been doing for the last few million years and the winds will blow without a care for the revelry or grief on earth.

'Our lungs and hearts will go on about their tasks as well – just the way they were doing for so many years; although I must add the liver, kidney and bladder might have to do some extra work for those who might have a few drinks extra,' he smiled at his own joke.

'I have figured that things are never as good or as bad as they appear. I realise people are good and bad inexplicably and our attempts to theorise about their goodness and vileness is futile. I realise that I have moments of spirited goodness and helpless meanness for no rhyme or reason – just like everyone else.

'I realise we look great or stupid alternatively, although some have some great runs for a longer period of time and others have the misfortune of a prolonged rough patch. This has got nothing to do with their talent, intent, hard work or any other factor that is within reasonable control. For no reason there are clouds and then suddenly for no reason there is sunshine.

'There is more randomness than destiny in the world and we should stop looking for cause and effect all the time.'

'Good happens to the wicked and shit happens to the good. In any case who is good and who is wicked keeps changing places just as what is good and what is shit also keeps changing.

'I realise there is more drama than sense around. I see the drama even as we talk about this topic locked in a hotel, a rich and educated guest asking a lowly hotel manager his views – it's no less than a drama, a drama that is both meaningful and inconsequential at the same time.

'I realise we are passengers in every conceivable way – on the earth, in the country, in the families, in the jobs and here in this hotel – I also realise we don't like being mere passengers. We want our journey to mean something. The more we realise that there is no meaning in it all, the more desperate is our need to seek meaning from every association, from every action, and from every event. I realise it is a wild goose chase.

'I realise that it is as bad not to have a purpose and perhaps it is much worse to be obsessively wedded to a purpose'

'So much is happening outside the window of the bus in which we are travelling. I realise that both have issues – not having a bus to call our own as well as belonging only to one bus. I realise moving and staying still have their own issues.

'I realise strange is not strange anymore – that strange is the new normal and that my own threshold for strangeness must improve significantly if I have to retain sanity and a sense of normalcy. Predictability is a myth – a mirage, a construct we have created because we don't know what we would do otherwise. It is better to chase an illusion that we can understand rather than live with reality that we cannot fathom. Reality never owed us anything and the illusion never had real teeth. We are doomed both ways.

'I realise that there is too much talk and too little action. I also realise that sometimes quick action is a substitute for deep thinking – it's a subterfuge by people who cannot think. Words are prison but so is action. Both can give us a false sense of accomplishment.

'I realise that there is only one human instinct above all - instinct to survive. Self-preservation is not only an art, but also a utility. So, when I see a blatant show of self-promotion or chicanery, of pettiness or vileness – I see a desperate attempt to survive. I do not get disturbed now when I see this. Something in me understands and allows it to be.

'*Sab moh maaya hai madam, sab moh maaya hai,*' Sunil ended.

The inmates of Hotel Landmark woke up that morning to further bad news. The number of infected in the world had crossed 12 lakhs and the dead was reaching 70,000. Closer home the number of dead was closing in on 150 and those testing positive was touching 5000. This pandemic was going berserk.

Prime ministers were getting infected, movie stars were not spared, the rich were dying and the poor were dying unceremoniously.

The poor countries were not able to stop it – the poor thought that they died only of hunger and deprivation. Little did they know that it does not matter how a poor person died. In fact, the poor die twice – they die every moment of their lives and then they die finally. It hardly makes a difference.

The war-ravaged countries were not able to stop it – countries which had fought communists, capitalists, imperialists and theologists for decades without giving up their resolve to fight, were giving up to a virus. The caliphate of their ambitions was crumbling in front of a tiny virus.

The rich countries were not able to stop it. They had all the resources and riches they could need; they had the confidence of decades of superiority, reinforced by some genuine progress and some fake vanity, and yet thousands were dying in their hospitals.

The old world was helpless, and the new world was helpless. The educated world was helpless; the uneducated world was helpless. Actually, in front of this mad pandemic there was only one world – a helpless world. *The helplessness had unified the world – perhaps for the first time.*

There was a bright side too. Human kindness and ingenuity were also at full display. The doctors and nurses were divine. They were serving like they had never served before, only more visibly this time. Food was being served to the needy; people were delivering medicines to the poor and the old. Money was being collected by businessmen, artists, and hell – even the politicians took a pay cut in some parts. *Corona managed to do what conscience had failed to achieve.*

There was rarely a time when there was so much despair and so much hope; both at the same time. Human mind was playing a seesaw – one moment filled with fear and anguish and the next moment filled with hope.

There was rarely a time when the world was so connected and yet it was difficult to believe that till only a few weeks ago, everyone was fighting with everyone else. The west fought the east, the left fought the right, the centre fought with itself, the rich fought with the poor, the atheist fought with the believer, one God's protectors fought with another God's protectors, while the Gods themselves Maybe having a jolly good time up in the heavens. Trade fought, business fought, capital fought. It was only now that every one of the above was fighting a common enemy – COVID-19.

Knowledge was being shared, medicines and technology were being shared, knowhow was being shared. Till only a few weeks ago everyone was busy erecting walls. A virus spoilt their plans. The world was connected in its grief, in its pain, in its danger of annihilation. Everyone was in this shit together – so far at least.

This world was suddenly a better version of itself thanks to a virus.

The dinner was about Old Monk, which incidentally now everyone had, and no one missed an opportunity to thank Sitam for his farsightedness in buying a crate.

The dinner was also about who will tell a story that day.

'I will tell a story my mother used to tell me in my village,' announced Sunil Paswan.

And Sunil told this story.

'My mother told me the story of a river – The river did not know how it really started. It had a vague memory that it started from the womb of a glacier before beginning its slow march downwards.

'Once she escaped out of the frozen confines, she started

to make her way down. She was tentative and unsure. She would test every rock, every gradient, every nook and every gap. She would begin by giving them a friendly nudge and if they would not listen, sometimes a violent push too. Some would not relent because they would be too big and obstinate. She was the newbie and those rocks had been around for a while. So, she would circle her way around those who obstructed her flow.

'She was young, and she had no time for debates. She would just circle around and move on, leaving the big rock exasperated and grumpy – large rocks usually looking for longer arguments.

'She would discover soon that those who do not have the freedom to move, or have a deep seated fear of moving on, or are just unable to move, or perhaps lack the imagination to move, prefer longer fights, even with smaller foes – for that is the only excitement in their lives. These small skirmishes bring them a semblance of joy in their otherwise stale lives. Those who can flow and move on, must be quick to move on. The young river was a smart cookie and that is exactly what she would do – avoid and move on. *Her moving on was more important to her than staying back to win the fight.*

'The river had no idea of the terrain or the flow in her initial days. As long as she was flowing down, she was content. She was not encumbered by the righteousness of a path – or *the* path. There was nothing in her mind called *the* path; all she was concerned with was *a* path. Any path that allowed her to move forward was good enough. In any case, the terrain she was flowing down from did not allow her the luxury of dealing with questions of righteousness. There was no time for it. She was too engrossed with the purpose of flowing. She was sure that she was right. She would deal with this question with a little less cockiness and certitude later in her course. *When you are young, being sure is more important.*

'She had gathered a great deal of speed and ferocity while she negotiated the turns and slopes of the mountains she passed through. While she credited herself with her speed, she also knew in her heart that sometimes our speed is also courtesy of the terrains we run through. Not everything is to our credit. She would be humbled very soon when she would hit the plains. In a lot of ways, she was not controlling her flow – the terrain was. She was just arrogant enough to take the entire credit.

'The change of flow of rivers do not announce themselves. All of a sudden, the terrain changed, and she was in the plains. Everything became excruciatingly slow. The sharp turns gave ways to a boring straight march ahead. Meandering became lazy at best. Gone was the turbulent flow, the impatient jump and the effervescent march. If she was to continue to move ahead, she needed poise, composure and patience. The terrain would not be of much help. Her own resolve, despite the languid pace and inadequate milestones, was the fuel of her journey. She was on her own now. Many rivers give up at this stage. They are not able to deal with the rhythm of slowness.

'*Slow has its own beauty*. It has its own cadence. Slow gives you time – time you can use to either ask fresh questions or take a hard look at your old answers. Slow allows pauses. A pause is often underrated. *We must celebrate pauses more often.*

'*The river which finally reaches the sea is the one which has survived the monotony of the plains*. Rivers need this one thing to reach their destination most – *resilience*. Staying put to the task of flowing is the only thing that matters.

'*Rivers need to have many facets and they must be good at all those facets if they want to have a rewarding run – in the hills powered by brute energy, and in the plains blessed with a matured doggedness, and finally at the mouth of the sea, an almost spiritual maturity on her good fortune.*'

'Be the river my son – my mother would often end the story,' Sunil said and went quiet.

16. A Heavy Day

Everyone woke up next morning to hear the news of the extension of the lockdown. They heard this piece of news with sinking spirits. Human mind on the matters of hope works in strange ways. *The finality of bad news is easier to deal with; but the news of a delay of good news or its reversal is unbearable.*

Everyone went about dealing with that bad news in their own way. The result was that not much conversation happened over food. *The first casualty of bad news is often human conversation. Happy people talk. Sad people just go quiet.*

There were two things that became apparent on the 15th day of the lockdown for those who cared to appreciate these things.

One, it became clear that when it comes to our mortal safety, religion ceases to matter – at least public displays of religion cease to matter for sure.

The paranoia of COVID was becoming shriller by the day. Almost everywhere mass religious gatherings had come to an end. Priests were doing Sunday mass alone, *aartis* and *abhisheks* in all major temples were done in isolation, daily rituals in *gurudwaras* and other places of worship were done privately or with very thin attendance. Finally, God was a personal subject. The usual hysteria about Him had taken second place – much after the subject of everyone's safety.

Not many would admit it – particularly by those for whom the public display of religiosity was a matter of pride and identity, but it was clear that God had become an extremely personal subject and the good news was that He did not mind it. All Gods had resolved that they will pretty much hold their court personally – one to one, direct from the worshipper to the worshipped. Most middlemen and conduits were sitting idle. The universe was running pretty well and there was hardly any evidence that either sins or sinners had increased because public display of religiosity had shrunk. Goodness, if at all, was at full display and more.

The second thing that also started to become clear was that politicians in general had receded from public attention, for at least those hundred stupid reasons for which they were highly visible. Apparently, their pet themes no longer peeved them these days. One wondered how long this self-administered celibacy of sorts would last for those motor mouths. The country was enjoying some respite.

Even the most powerful were in the request mode – whether the request was to chant, light or applaud, but at least it was a request. Many chief ministers were apologising for the discomfort they had put their citizens through. If it were not for these circumstances, it would have been impossible to imagine that it was our country, and these were our leaders!

Distance exposes cracks in relationships. It sometimes also reveals all that is magical. And with sufficient time one discovers both. All five in Hotel Landmark were experiencing distance from their families for the first time and discovering the deepest cracks and the strongest glue. The only thing that they were not very sure of was which was the crack, and which was the glue.

People stay together for a long time for very strange reasons – sometimes, for all that is perfect between them and sometimes for all the cracks in them.

Sitam realised that he was too engrossed in his dissatisfaction – of not having achieved enough, not commensurate to what he thought he deserved. He sulked alone; he drank alone. He directed the anger that he felt at his life not turning out the way he wanted it to, towards himself. The more he kept his frustration to himself, the more that loneliness fed on itself. Soon his tendency to constantly stay with himself had consumed his relationships – wife and son.

Sitam realised one fine day that distance had creeped in. Two boats had drifted apart. The boats had not actively rowed away from each other, but the waves had made them drift apart. He realised that relationships are like such boats on water – they have to be tied to each other to keep them together. If you did not do anything to stay together, the waves would take you away and apart from each other. He realised he had allowed a gradual weakening of his relationships in his decision to deal with his grief alone. He had forgotten that grief brings people together like no other emotion. He did not like to share his anguish and in the pursuit of saving his relationships from his pain, he had created a distance that he no longer knew how to fill. *Shared pain sometimes keeps relationships together.*

Kulwant realised that she had grown apathetic towards her loved ones. Her grief was the deep hurt she nursed of her victimhood – the feeling that she had been used. She felt a seething rage at the very thought that she was used all these years. So strong was her repulsion towards everyone that she ignored all that was good in her life, all that had been good in her life. She was beginning to realise that it was no one's fault that her life felt empty now. Her husband was not responsible for most things that she nursed in her heart as a colossal void. *Often there is no culprit for our pains. We make those who are available as culprits.*

Kulwant realised she had been looking for gratitude all these years, more than anything else. In the past few days she was coming to terms with the futility of that need. No one owes any thankfulness to us. Our desire for it is our vanity and a needless burden on our loved ones. The way our lives turn out to be is a random event. Our parents don't have any control in choosing us nor do we have any control over choosing them, our spouses and children are similarly random in their presence in our lives and our presence in theirs. Everyone does their best. *When we experience gratitude – that is the best in us as human beings; when we expect gratitude, that is the worst.*

Manoj became aware of his self-centredness over this period of being alone. He understood many parts of his fights with his wife. He realised that all these years it had been all about him and him alone. His need for importance, his need for success, his need for validation, his need for victory and his need to have the last word was always all about him. So high was his presence in a relationship that there was no space for anyone else. Anyone with him was doomed from day one. He almost felt surprised that his wife was still with him after all these years.

He realised that even the smallest hint of correction or advice or feedback from anyone was anathema to him. It was as if something started to happen the moment someone suggested a correction to him. He almost started to hate that side of him. He did not like his own awareness of himself. Nothing can be worse than that. *We can deal with the world telling us about what is wrong with us; when we figure that out ourselves, we are filled with disgust.*

His instinct was to fight this realisation and then he cursed himself a little more – fighting with self is infinitely more difficult than fighting with others.

Razia had started to realise her hollowness. She was becoming aware of how her life meant nothing at all. She realised that having all the money to take care of herself and enjoying all the finer things in life was not enough. There must be a grand purpose to it – as grand as one can make it. The grandeur need not be glamourous, but it must be as grand as there is a potential for it to be.

She became aware that Srijith was a not a maverick in working with the poorest – he found meaning in his work. She became painfully aware of how little meaning her life had had so far, how little purpose! It was not enough not to need less, you had to mean something to others. There was a word for someone who only lived for themselves – parasite.

Sunil became aware that his life had slipped by while protecting himself and his loved ones. He did not have a choice in being born in those circumstances in that village in Bihar or the circumstances under which he had to run away from it – or the many years he had spent on the singular task of surviving. He realised that those days had mercifully passed. He had no need to run anymore. His big realisation was that he was still running, and he was still in that village.

Despite his thirty years in Mumbai he had still not become a Mumbaikar. He was pained by his own shameless ingratitude towards the city, its people and Hotel Landmark.

In the lives of the inmates of Hotel Landmark, Day 15 of the COVID-19 lockdown took a lot longer to pass than what it takes for a day to pass.

17. The Cottage Industry called Love

If the 15th day appeared longer than usual, then the 16th day would appear as never-ending.

When everyone came down to have breakfast, they found the usually vivacious Sunil Paswan forlorn and quiet. Only after a lot of prodding he shared that his wife had called to say that she was suffering from cough and was running a temperature for the last day or two. They were suspecting the worst.

Sunil had tried to console his wife as best as he could, but he was fearful.

Despair is the biggest epidemic. It spreads faster than the epidemic itself. Hope flies away in the face of fear faster than the blink of an eye.

These were times when even the slightest news could flare up. A small cough and a sneeze had the power to scare people. It was not logical but the odds of dying of an accident and diabetes or a heart attack was a hundred times more, but people were more scared of catching the infection. Fear is irrational. It was not surprising that Sunil was only thinking of the worst. It could be a mere flu or an ordinary fever – but nothing was ordinary in the times of mass hysteria. He was worried for his wife for multiple reasons – one, of course that it could be the COVID itself, but more importantly he wondered how she would cope with that fear alone.

Dying in a matter of moments is the best way of going. A sudden accident or breathing your last while asleep is an end that comes only to the blessed. One would not be contemplating the thought of death while dying. Normally we think of death so many times while being alive that it appears that we have died a hundred times even before we actually die.

Those who suffer from disability or disease suffer the worst. One knows that one is hurtling towards the precipice irrevocably, either with speed or in slow motion. Every moment for such a person is equal to dying because the thought of dying is as bad as dying, maybe worse.

There is a situation that is even worse than that – and Sunil Paswan's heart shred into pieces to think that his wife would be going through that – she would not know if she was safe, or should she fear the worst!

She would be vacillating between extreme hope and extreme despair. Every swing from one extreme to another would be excruciating and so draining.

At one moment the heart hopes everything to be normal, that one should be safe, and the very next moment one would fall into the dark dungeons of despair, thinking of only the worst.

Swinging from extreme hopefulness to rabid fear is a hundred times worse than a fear which is constant. A fear that we know is *fait accompli* can actually cease to matter after a while. Life and our minds can adjust to the idea of even mortality if we know it is certain. In a way, we do not fear death as much as we fear uncertainty.

The whole day Sunil kept on swinging from the extremes of hope to fear. It would take the hotel owner a few hours to arrange his replacement and Sunil to make necessary arrangements to take his wife to the doctor and the testing centre by the evening.

The four guests also got affected by this news. They got affected in ways they did not imagine they would – after all it was merely the wife of the manager of the hotel they were incidentally staying in during the lockdown.

They perhaps did not know this about Grief. It is contagious too.

Sitam suddenly became fearful of staying away from family. He suffered a bout of fear for his son and his wife who were alone in their respective places. It dawned upon him, there was only one thing worse than having your family in some kind of danger – that the family is facing that danger alone. Your presence may not make any material difference to that danger, but the fact that you are together is a relief. If your family has to go through the worst, then you prefer that they do so in your presence.

Kulwant realised that the fear of death makes you forgive far more easily. One can carry grudges for decades and sometimes even for one's entire life, promising oneself not to forget or forgive – but a news of impeding death changes the equation. *A grudge loses its potency in the face of the possibility of death.* All such complaints and grudges appear puny and petty.

One wants to reconcile before dying – settle accounts. One wants to say sorry, admit love and mistakes and let bygones be bygones. It's funny that all of that could have been done ordinarily too but one is too vain and haughty to do it. *Death reminds us of our pettiness and the meaninglessness of our grudges.*

The more one witnesses the canvas of artists, the span of cinema, the depths of poetry and the expanse of prose, the more one gets convinced that the story of human sensibilities is shaped by the stories of love and its various forms of *unfulfilment.*

When two people talk about love, specifics do not matter and honestly no one remembers them because maybe they do not matter. Yet two complete strangers can connect through a piece of art or a song or a movie, because angst or pathos unites the creator and the observer. All love stories we remember are stories of unfulfillment – Kulwant concluded in an amazing moment of clarity.

So, what is it that makes it so much talked about, so much written about, so much mused about – this whole thing about love attaining some kind of permanence?

She concluded that it was the impossible utopia about love that made it popular in everyone's imagination. Everyone knows that utopia does not exist, but its pursuit is seductive. *The idea of love is so pure in its construct, that there is inspiration even in the failure to find it.*

Manoj heard the news about Sunil's wife and went into silence. He thought of death for the first time. He thought of the prospect of not seeing someone you love ever again. He wondered how come this thought had never occurred to him, only to realise that people full of themselves often don't get this so easily.

Time with people is precious because it is limited. No one knows which moment is the last one. The vanity of those who are obsessed with winning, is to believe that even in relationships winning is victory. They forget in the duels with those whom you love, that winning happens because there exists a duel. No duel means no more winning. One must wish that the duels continue long enough. *Death means there is no one left to fight.*

Razia was lost. She was getting used to the idea of death. She realised that love and such sundry afflictions of the heart are lofty ideals, sometimes too lofty and too pompous. Love needs life to blossom. The ultimate sign of growing up is coming to terms with the idea that our stay with people we love is limited. Razia came face-to-face with this reality for the first time in her life – and perhaps for the first time she realised that growing up is not a pleasant experience.

Sunil left for his home to attend to the matters of his family. They did not know this yet, but Sunil will come back later to create an upheaval in their lives, that they in their current state cannot even imagine. They shall also remain forever indebted to him for that.

Someone else joined in place of him. It was not their Sunil.

Day 16 in the life of a country in lockdown did not bring in much hope. The number of deaths continued to march ahead – they stood at 205 and more than 6000 reported infected. The global number was far more depressing –

almost 90,000 dead and more than 15 lakh infected. The national government had given clear indications that this lockdown would go beyond the 21 days. Orissa had officially declared so. Karnataka and Maharashtra were almost at the edge of declaring so. Life in the country as the citizens knew it had stopped.

No one wished for more time at home, with family and children. No one talked of work-life balance anymore – it was unlikely that any of them would speak of these things for many more years. Human grief is a lot like amoeba – it constantly changes shape.

18. Death Talks to Us

The news of the possibility of Sunil Paswans wife's COVID infection had jolted everyone at Hotel Landmark, also because suddenly, the virus scare was at their doorstep.

We have a strange relationship with scares, things that announce apocalypse, the end of the world. It's either very near or very far away in our imagination and hence the fear of it is either very palpable that we can feel it in our bones or too distant to scare us. We have a dichotomous relationship with such scares.

For most believers in some kind of religion, the fear of that apocalypse comes along with the promise of heavenly bliss. It's the carrot and stick – they often go together. Hence, we know that the end of the world is very near or very far depending upon the strength of our faith. The deeper the faith, the more are the chances of the believer experiencing that scare in her soul.

Atheists and non - believers are far removed from such joys and scares. Their minds can imagine neither.

Then there are fears of climactic apocalypse, the rising sea water levels consuming our coastal cities, or melting glaciers creating havoc or rising pollution destroying the fragile ecosystem, irreparably damaging our food chains.

It does not end there. There have been stories about technology overpowering humans and aliens becoming our masters. There are hundreds of such stories. For most of us, these do not touch us beyond arousing a cursory interest.

The reason is that we lack the ability to feel fear till it knocks on our doors. We have to see its ghoulish face to believe the havoc it can create. We have to see the diseased to understand morbidity, we have to see the mutilated to understand disability, we have to see destruction to understand its havoc, we have to see death to realise our innate mortality. In a way all of us live completely unmindful of the true nature of life. Each one of us lives in a cocoon. Only the nature of the cocoon differs. The role of the cocoon remains the same – keep reality at bay.

However, death talks to us. We either don't listen to it or don't remember what it says long enough.

The mere suspicion that the deadly Corona had reached the home of someone they knew was when it really hit them – *that this was all real.*

The lockdown was a physical discomfort and nothing more than that. They hated its imposition, but it did not alarm them the way this news had done. They were surprised every time they read the news of people breaking the lockdown curbs or groups of people coming together in utter disregard for their own safety and the safety of others – a part of their minds actually empathised with them, if not condoned them.

'After all how long can someone be stuck in the confines of their homes – if some of them have come out momentarily, it might have broken the curbs of law, but it was not a huge crime, it was not a huge danger,' they had rationalised often.

However, now it hit them with a sledgehammer because death had knocked on the doors of someone they knew. COVID was not merely a news item anymore – it was much more, and much closer – they could feel its fear far more intimately.

Death becomes a fear only with such intimacy – otherwise death is a stranger.

Manoj felt an acute need to bring life back into their conversations. So, at lunch that day he began by sharing stuff that he was watching on the net.

'You know, I chanced upon this very fascinating story about a group of seven children. In the year 1964 ITV, a British station commissioned a documentary featuring, fourteen children all aged seven, picked up from a cross-section of backgrounds, to represent a slice of British life.'

'What about that documentary?' asked Razia, not sounding too enthused.

'The interesting thing is that the director, Michael, on his part did not stop at that. Ever since 1964 he has gone back to those fourteen kids every seven years, a good nine times and tried to capture those lives till they reached age 63 and how those lives have turned out,' he said.

Now Razia was getting slightly more interested, 'you mean those seven strangers were brought back every seven years? They would be quite old now, wouldn't they?'

'Yes – they are 63 now,' confirmed Manoj. 'How life would have changed for them every seven years – I find the idea very fascinating.

'Let's play this,' said Manoj. 'Let's begin at age seven and check how our lives have progressed.'

'Ok,' said Razia, not too sure how this game would evolve but still wanting to play along.

She also wanted to get everyone together for some exciting conversation. The story sharing sessions had come to an abrupt end and she realised the banter and the camaraderie had begun to suffer.

'Companionship does not develop in isolation' – she thought. 'It demands people do things together, read, talk, tell stories, play games, cook, take a walk, draw! It does not matter how exalted or how stupid – the trick is to do things together. Even if it's a wastage of time now, that is the only thing that stays as memories – you need stories in old age to talk about.' *Those who do not have stories to tell die prematurely or live painfully.*

Razia began. 'Let me go first. Let me begin how it was when I was seven. Seven was an age of wanting things, eating favourites, sleeping peacefully and snuggling in the warmth of parents' love, knowing and believing that is the most secure place in the world, and will remain so forever.'

Manoj continued – 'Fourteen for me was the age of wanting to grow up fast and have more freedom, of wanting to be accepted and liked, of looking at adults with envy, for their strength, youth, vigour and their freedom to be able to take their own decisions.'

Sitam understood the game by now. He picked up the baton – 'Twenty-one for me was the age to look good, have even more freedom, particularly more money and the decision where to spend it. It would also be the age of envy and a few heartbreaks. Believing in ideals would come naturally to me and there was a happily thereafter in all things. The idea of everlasting youth, everlasting love and everlasting happiness was the driving idealism.'

Kulwant joined now, 'Twenty-eight for me was the year of idealism. The body had bloomed fully, the mind was ready to take on all challenges and the heart was ready to let come all that was beautiful. There was beauty in small things and large, and being swept off my feet was not only possible but also constantly desired.'

'Now what?' Asked Razia because everyone had got a chance.

'We go to round two and continue,' – suggested Manoj.

Razia continued – 'Thirty-five is the age when a rhythm has set in or at least it would appear that way. There is the onset of the feeling of growing up too fast. The burden of responsibilities has started to interfere with small joys and an early realization is gnawing – that one cannot have it all, that one has to make choices. A few scars have been earned by now.'

Everyone noticed that she spoke in the present tense.

Manoj picked up from there, 'Forty-two is the age when it has first dawned that half of life as I know it is well behind me. Joys are muted and celebrations are not as much fun as they used to be. Cynicism is fully formed. Ageing parents are difficult to accept. The rose-tinted idealism of I-can-have-it-all has started to fray either at its margins or at its core. Being a believer in things, people and relationships is taking more and more effort.'

Another present tense. It was not a game after all. It was clear that everyone was telling their own story.

It was Sitam's chance, 'Forty-nine is when it hits hard. The greys in the temple have emerged, the furrows on the head have started to show and with that also attempts to conceal them in any which way have increased. Friends start to appear old and jaded, overweight and balding, silly and repetitive.'

Kulwant continued, 'Fifty-six is when you are decisively old, whether you accept it or not. Children defy you and I do not quite recognize the ways of the world anymore. I want the old order back, *not because it was better but only because it was familiar*. The body is showing signs of ageing in many possible ways. Regrets are more than dreams and mortality has become amply obvious. *The flame flickers brighter in one last desperate attempt.*'

This was present continuous, and it hit everyone.

Everyone kept quiet. How it would look to be at 63 was known to only one person at the table and they did not want to mock this very serious game now by hazarding a guess.

Kulwant understood the silence and continued.

'Sixty-three is the age of finally questioning the meaning of it all. It is the time for taking stock and asking if it was a life well-lived and worth living. Even though many years are still left, I am asking if living itself is worth it. I am asking questions about follies and forgiveness, principles and lack of them, of too much patience or the lack of it, or too much faith or the lack of it, of too much importance to things that had not mattered and too little to those that did matter. *Rear-view has become more important than the road ahead.'*

She was quiet. Others were quiet. There was a quietness around like never before.

19. The Burden of Pettiness

It was difficult to believe that it was already 18 long days since the lockdown had begun. It did not feel like 18 days. It appeared as if it was only yesterday that they were dealing with the shock of what it meant to be trapped within four walls. It was a surprise that they had survived 18 days. Only 3 more days to go. Freedom felt so near.

Yet everything that they were hearing, and reading was contrary to that. They knew that this lockdown would in all likelihood, get extended. While all wanted safety, the likelihood of this extension did not feel like welcome news, definitely not by the four guests stuck in Hotel Landmark.

For the past 18 days most individuals and families had been living in such physically constrained proximity for the first time in their living memory. This was not something anyone was used to or prepared for. Frankly speaking, nobody is prepared for something like this.

An element of freedom is a necessity for relationships and families to function properly. Even those who do not go out for a job have respite during the day when the rest go out. That respite was no longer available to both. They also realised what critical role such respite had played so far in keeping the families together.

Most would not have said it aloud out of politeness and also because it sounded offensive - but everyone had realised through this lockdown that staying together 24 x 7 this long was the surest way to kill love between individuals and families. No amount of love can withstand this kind of proximity. *Love needs some lies, some half lies, and some distance to flourish.*

A prolonged proximity also amplifies the cracks in relationships. You start to become more acutely aware of all that is so irritating in people you are in love with – spouses, children and parents. You stare at even the most well painted wall long enough, even the smallest of cracks will become visible. Families were going through this awareness. They were still upholding the pretence of eternal love because breaking that pretence would kill them faster than the virus.

Love also needs the glorious role play of pretences. If everyone starts to speak the truth all the time, there would be no intact relationships left on earth left. *Human lives are built on the foundation of this subterfuge.*

In fact, this subterfuge is so prevalent and so ubiquitous that it appears normal. This lying or half lying does not appear out of ordinary. In fact, it does not even qualify as lying in our minds. Our truths are determined by the narratives in our minds, mostly the false narratives repeated so many times that they appear to be the truth. Eighteen days of such intense proximity had made it impossible to bear the burden of hiding this subterfuge.

The society was not really fighting the battle of the pandemic waiting to explode – the real danger the society was battling, was what this prolonged proximity had exposed in relationships. *Now everyone knew how utterly intolerable in most parts they all were to each other.*

If those stuck with their loved ones were facing the problems of noticing the cracks in what lay between them and their loved ones, the guests in Hotel Landmark in Mumbai had begun to notice what bound them with their family. *If extreme proximity is bad news, then a prolonged distance once in a while is a blessing.*

These guests had started to realise that finally, love was nothing more than sharing time together – its small moments and its large.

Finally, love was the ability to talk to each other for a few hours in a day without feeling compelled to kill each other. Love was thankfulness that there was someone in the room who could understand our silences and with whom we had the liberty to be silent and yet be understood. It is always difficult to define what love is; *love is what love does.*

It is a feeling that at the end of the day makes you feel that you are not alone. They say that the opposite of love is not hate but apathy – the presence of love can be ascertained by only one feeling – that you do not feel alone.

Only the utterly lonely know how much more death is preferred over loneliness.

'Any news of Sunil's wife?' asked Razia. 'Has anyone called him?'

'I had,' said Manoj. All were quite surprised that amongst all of them it was Manoj who had called to check up on Sunil.

Espousing care and empathy are not necessarily the same as demonstrating them. Sometimes the most sensitive acts come from the coldest and seemingly self-centred people and at other times the most sensitive people can demonstrate a ruthless and cold-hearted streak. All of us *are layers of contradictions held together precariously and inexplicably.*

'He said that they had managed to take her to a hospital, and she had been tested for COVID – results were awaited.'

'Hope all is good,' said Kulwant quite concerned. 'I read that Mumbai is actually the worst hit so far. The highest dead and the highest infected are from Maharashtra and Mumbai in particular.

'Yup. 1660 infected and 110 out of the 253 dead are from here,' commented the ever-knowledgeable MBA, Manoj.

'The worst thing is that a large number of frontline health workers like doctors and nurses are increasingly being infected in Mumbai. There are so many hospitals that have been closed.' said Kulwant.

'Right again. Some big names like Jaslok Hospital, Wockhart, Bhatia Hospital and some smaller ones are all closed and quarantined,' once again chipped in Manoj.

'What about other places?' asked Kulwant to no one in particular.

'Bad situation. More than 250 dead, more than 7500 reportedly infected in India. And worldwide it is even scarier – more than a lakh dead and more than 17 lakhs infected.

'Actually, we do not realise how safe we have been

here in this hotel,' spoke Sitam for the first time in this conversation.

Everyone agreed.

None of them could have known that all the comfort and sense of protection they were experiencing at that moment would get shattered by the evening. No one knew that they would come face-to-face with their own ugly side soon. They would soon see the reflection of their souls and what would stare back at them would not be kind to their vanity. They would realise that beneath the veneer of civility and the image of good human beings they were as rotten and broken as anyone else.

Late in the afternoon the new manager called all of them down to the dining area and informed them that the owner and the local government authorities had decided to convert the hotel into a temporary stay facility for all the doctors, nurses and health workers who were working on the frontlines of the COVID pandemic in that locality. They were informed that these people would start using the hotel from that very night.

The four guests almost flew into a rage against the hotel manager. All kinds of arguments were used by them

'Isn't this highly irresponsible towards us? By allowing all of them to stay here you are putting all of us in grave mortal risk.'

'Look, we appreciate the work these doctors and nurses are doing – but we also know that they are also at the highest risk. We would be constantly living in fear if they start to live here.'

'Could you not have moved them to a hotel where there are no other guests – or at least move us to those locations?'

'It is highly unprofessional.'

It was many hours after the hotel manager left that this discussion tapered. All his arguments about being socially responsible and rising up to the occasion and service to the nation fell on deaf years. They understood what he was trying to say, even appreciated it, but still could not agree to being comfortable with the idea.

The four recognised something deeply poignant in themselves that day. They realised that beneath their skin they were extremely self-centered and selfish. They realised that admiring the professions in service to the nation and service to society in cocktail parties, on social media and even speaking from podiums, is one thing – but things change when you are at personal risk.

Soldiers look great in Republic Day parades, movies and the jingoism on the Facebook wall and the Twitter thread – but donning fatigues or sending your son to do it is difficult.

It is easy to clap from balconies and blow conch shells for the brave work that the health workers were doing but living with them every evening when they returned from that war is scary. They realised how hollow their lives were.

They realised that they knew things cognitively but did not have the strength of the soul to live the values they espoused.

Some concepts reveal themselves to us as epiphanies while some others remain at a cognitive level. We often mistake cognitive appreciation as the final frontier. However, things must come alive to really make a difference.

The chasm between what should be and what is, is tragic and ironic at the same time – and when it's neither, it is funny.

The esoteric subjects like social service, service to nation, leadership, social change, cultural progress *et al* are all subjects that suffer from this chasm – and in Hotel Landmark that evening, that chasm, depressing as it was, was on glorious display.

It would take them many more years to realise how depressingly ordinary and petty they sounded that evening. Each one would have that realisation in different ways and under different circumstances. Some would not have it at all.

If conversations about self-awareness cause a heightened self-awareness, most of us would be saints.

That day they realised something new – *The futility of knowledge*. Knowing, mostly means nothing.

The rest of the days in Hotel Landmark were not the same anymore. One, it started to appear like a hospital more than a hotel. All conversations revolved around COVID, all the time.

Second, except them, there was no one there who seemed to be overwhelmed by the danger of working through perhaps the greatest danger of our times. The four guests were surprised at the joviality, the banter, the general bonhomie amongst all the new arrivals. If they did not know, it would appear that these guys were working in a mall and not fighting a deadly virus. If there was a larger purpose that was driving them, it was definitely not being talked about – they were going about their jobs as a matter of fact. They looked ordinary, talked ordinary and behaved ordinary. They could have been anyone.

That last thing hit the four original guests the hardest. Even those who are out there saving the world and doing such altruistic and higher order things were ordinary human beings. Nothing about them would have given away their greatness – and yet what they were doing, day in and day out, despite huge personal risks, was nothing short of extraordinary.

All four of them wondered what made people great and how come they were so petty and self-centered. This question would start to gnaw at their souls that evening onwards – and slowly and gradually it would eat away at their peace of mind.

They would find the burden of this pettiness unbearable on their souls. None of them could call out this burden, define it, put it in words and express it – but they felt it pounding heavily in their hearts and hitting them like a thousand cannon balls.

No human soul is more traumatised than the one which has to see his own pettiness in the mirror.

They would not get the answer to this question for many more days. They will have to wait for some more time in the lockdown to taste liberation.

20. No Miracles for Stupidity

The chances were remote that even the most die-hard believers of faith believed that Gods were on their side during the times of Covid.

It was *Ramnavmi* on 2nd April, the birth celebration of the God who symbolises the ultimate standard a human being could achieve.

It was *Mahavir Jayanti* on the 6th of April, the celebration of the profound conversion of an ordinary human being into the state of perfection through self-realisation.

It was *Hanuman Jayanti* on the 8th, the symbol of strength, loyalty, service and above all, dependability.

It was *Good Friday*, a day of penance on the 10th and then there was *Easter*, the day symbolising resurrection, where the ordinary dies to create something more meaningful.

It did not end there.

The 13th-14th of April marked the beginning of the New Year in the traditional Solar calendar. The country celebrated its New Year's – from *Vaisakhii* in Punjab, *Pana Sankranti* in Odisha, *Pohela Boishakh* in West Bengal, *Vishu* in Kerala and *Puthandu* in Tamil Nadu respectively.

On the 26th of the month during the extended lockdown, the country celebrated *Akshaya Tritiya*, the festival of "never diminishing wealth, prosperity and happiness."

At least the Indian believers could not have been armed with better ammunition than this. If ever the battle of good and evil was to be fought with support from the heavens above, this was the best possible time. There was almost a celestial bonanza unleashed against the virus.

There was a poignant difference between the old guests and the new ones in Hotel Landmark.

The older guests did not notice what their scriptures had preached in circumstances such as these because they were too worried and engrossed about their own safety.

The new guests did not care much about such celestial ammunition – *they were the ammunition.*

Faith in old Gods or no faith, it was clear that everyone needed a new beginning. It was high time. If someone would have told them that the way you could miraculously get rid of this problem was to reject your old Gods, old beliefs, and old festivals, chances are that a large majority would have at least considered the idea, if not immediately accepted it.

Diminishing hope from existing Gods is a fertile time for new Gods to emerge.

The day also delivered bad news – that Sunil's wife was indeed detected with COVID. She had been shifted to a hospital. They checked with Sunil to see how he was coping – he sounded in control. Even if he was rattled it was difficult to make it out from his voice. Maybe he was not as scared as they feared. A man who has gone through the violence perpetrated by fellow human beings is often not rattled by the ones unleased by nature. The violence of nature makes you anguished but not angry; violence of human beings makes you choke with rage.

Kulwant, Sitam, Manoj and Razia had made a few acquaintances ever since the doctors and nurses came to Hotel Landmark and they would make many more every time they would come down. Almost every one of them would leave them amazed.

They met doctors who had not gone to their homes for the last 19 days. One of them had been blessed with a newborn while he was serving patients. He had not seen the baby girl, whose arrival he had so been looking forward to. They met doctors who had not slept for days together, napping in wards and small beds, eating whatever they got – till Hotel Landmark allowed them to come and rest there. They were sleeping in normal clean beds, taking baths and wearing proper clothes after a long time.

They met nurses and other paramedic staff who were coming from even worse conditions. They often lived in cramped hostels and poor localities of Mumbai. They were the dark underbelly of the medical profession, where if any recognition ever came, often came to the doctors. The nurses, the cleaners, the housekeeping were the dregs that no one noticed and rarely acknowledged.

The four guests in Hotel Landmark heard stories after stories of these unsung heroes and heroines who were battling the COVID nightmare without any concern for their own safety and comfort whatsoever. They heard stories of their hunger, lack of sleep, lack of sanitation, exhaustion and most importantly the huge burden of responsibility they carried – but never once did they hear them complain or express fear.

It was clear to them that none of these were the most well-paid or lived a life of high means. It was clear that all of them carried exactly the same notions of success in their heads – of owning the best and the latest, of acquiring homes, cars and jewellery, of holidays and weekends, of chilling and letting their hair down. The four guests, however, could not find even one trace of regret in any one of these warriors.

What baffled the four guests most about these people was how they were so happy and relaxed! Each found a different and yet, a common answer.

Sitam figured out that they seemed to love what they did. More than the money, comfort or the power a profession indicated in the social hierarchy of professions, these people were in it for the sheer joy of what they were achieving through their work.

The cleaner was not just a cleaner and a nurse was not just a nurse and a doctor was not just a doctor – each one of them was a little more than the things they did. In normal circumstances they may not have realised it but now they did. In normal circumstances maybe they would have grudged others their lifestyle or the money others made and may have cursed themselves for their chosen professions – but not anymore.

Film stars, businessmen, high flying executives, powerful politicians and bureaucrats were all lining in front of them with only one appeal in their eyes – *save us*! Sitam realised that the pride in their own work that each one of them was experiencing since the Corona scare broke out would be enough to carry them for the rest of their lives. Never again will others consider them cogs in a machine and never again will they look at others with eyes of regret. Sitam had never felt the same way ever about working in bureaucracy.

Kulwant arrived at a similar conclusion albeit from a different route. She realised how critical it is to realise the utility of your work. Sometimes it takes a crisis to make this utility abundantly clear. She had always questioned her accomplishment as a home maker. She was beginning to realise that keeping the house anchored and raising children was no less a profound achievement of her life, than the achievement of her husband or her children. *Their successes stood on her shoulders, so as to be visible to the world.* She had never felt prouder of herself than in that moment.

Razia and Manoj felt small and petty – albeit for different reasons.

Razia felt incomplete because she felt like a dry leaf floating in the air. She did not know what was the worth of her life. She felt incomplete.

Some pursue achievement for meaning, some pursue a larger good – she had pursued nothing. She felt like a parasite – who has only taken from others, first from parents, then from Srijith but never given back. If she were to die today nothing would be amiss even in one soul's life. She thought of Srijith's life and how he had devoted his entire being for the betterment of those who were in need. She felt even more incomplete. Even more painfully in this moment she also felt quite undeserving of her comforts, and more importantly, she felt undeserving of Srijith.

Manoj was shattered. All his 'Engineer-MBA from the best colleges of the country' pride was exposed to be just that – *useless pride*. He realised that his tribe were modern day narcissists, driven only by the hunger to build for themselves. Even when they were building companies, they were building partly, if not completely, for themselves.

The drive was rarely about how much they would give – to their organisations, society and people, it was always about what they would get. He questioned the entire notion of the purpose of enterprise and within that the motives of his own ambitions. He wanted to believe that all his intelligence, suave articulation, his smartness, his evolved sense of logic and erudition meant something. He was no longer sure of it.

The more he interacted with all these people fighting the Covid battle the more he realised that all his accomplishments surely meant a lot to him, but they did not mean even a tiny bit to anyone else. What bore a hole in his soul was not that his profession seemed so meaningless in comparison to the vocation of the people he was staying with – what really hit him was the bloated sense of importance he had been living his life with so far. He realised what a hoax his life was and what a great imposter he had been. *Nothing is more painful than the agony of recognising your own bullshit.*

Every time they met during the day; all they could talk about was the greatness they witnessed around them. Each one of them talked about one more doctor, one more nurse and one more paramedic staff – and shared the details of his or her story. Their own inadequacy, their own smallness was always the unsaid but completely understood. It was clear to each one of them, but none had the courage to admit it.

However, there was one definite advantage to the constant telling and retelling of these stories, although it was not apparent to them yet, that they were reaching a tipping point, at which time they will be left with no choice but to take a decision. At some stage they had to come to terms with the sham of a life they were living and perhaps from that disgrace would emerge the courage to do something about it. *True transformation mostly emerges only after a steep fall from grace.*

Most human inspiration emerges from gross inadequacy, from feeling small and incomplete, from feeling helpless even. The inspiration however comes much later – first you have to go through the anguish of that inadequacy, incompleteness and helplessness. Most people never come out of that stage because it is tormenting and excruciating; hence most people never live inspired or inspiring lives. *They are first consumed by their pain and then condemned by it.*

There was an unintended consequence of this anguish that the four original guests of Hotel Landmark were going through. It however went completely unnoticed by all of them – they were no longer visibly worried about the prospect of being stuck here anymore.

Hotel Landmark on the 19th day of the lockdown was a beehive of activity – so was the country. It was almost certain that the lockdown would be extended by two more weeks.

The number of deaths in India was around 280 and counting with 8650 reported cases. Strange stories had also emerged. An Orissa youth had cycled more than 1700 kilometres from Maharashtra and was finding that being stuck in the house was more difficult than cycling for that long. A mother in Hyderabad had rode more than 1400 kilometres to bring back her son. The crown however went to the case where a person sneaked in a friend to his apartment in a suitcase, because they desperately needed company.

If the funny did not stop, neither did the stupid. There were incidents where people were still defying the lockdown and not heeding the instructions for social distancing.

The powerful did that because of arrogance, the poor did that because of necessity; some did out of ignorance and most did it out of stupidity.

Most Gods in the eyes of the believers can solve almost anything through their miracles. However, what no one realised was that none of the Gods whose birthdays or resurrections or even the auspicious planetary positions they had celebrated recently were powerful enough to solve the problems of human stupidity.

21. The Earthworm and the Gazelle

The lockdown did extend and so did their misery.

Over the course of the coming days each one of them met people who would leave them profoundly touched and deeply jolted.

Kulwant and Manoj were together when they met Srinath Walke. He would be 65. He was working as a paramedic staff in the hospital. He looked older than everyone else. He shared that when the chief minister called for retired medical staff to return to service to fight the COVID menace, he came out of his retirement. He had retired some five years back from the Nair Hospital in Mumbai where he was the ward attendant in the Operation Theatre. His job was to do the most menial of the tasks in the most critical part of the hospital.

He had been enjoying his retired life with his son who was a mid-level executive in a leading private sector bank, when he heard about the call by the chief minister. He decided to come back to serve yet again in this moment of crisis.

Kulwant and Manoj could not understand the old man or his motivations. There was no logical reason why this old man, having given his entire life to the struggles of keeping the fires burning in his kitchen, having done the lowliest of low jobs, had now returned to do perhaps the most dangerous work of his life, especially when he had no reason or compulsion to do it!

They could not resist asking him. Srinath looked at these two people intently to understand the question they were asking of him. If he appeared an enigma to them, they in turn appeared dumb to him. For him – this was a non-question.

He had met these kinds who considered living for a higher ideal naivety at best and stupidity at worst. His own son was like them – who had not quite fathomed why his father had to return to do this. In a way, this conversation was happening in his life for the second time.

So, he chose to tell them a story. He hoped a story would explain it better for them than his explanation had worked for his son.

'There was a gazelle and an earthworm,' Srinath began.

'Can you hurry please?' asked the gazelle to the earthworm. The young earthworm could only smile. The earthworm did not know that even if he was fast in the earthworm sense, he would always be slow in comparison to the grasshopper, who in turn would not know what being fast like a gazelle was.

'Being fast or slow is such a strange thing. When an earthworm and a gazelle talk about being slow or fast, one would forgive both for not knowing or understanding each other. The earthworm would have to be a gazelle and the gazelle would have to be an earthworm for that to happen, and since that is unlikely, they would have to reconcile to not knowing what being slow and fast really meant to each other.

'Why can't you slow down please?' asked the earthworm to the gazelle, this time with a smile. The gazelle also smiled back. She knew that no gazelle had ever known slowing down. Gazelles were known to run, hop and scamper all the time, sometimes in joy and other times to save themselves from predators.

'I will be hunted down if I slowed down,' said the gazelle. One could not have argued with her fear. It is a fear that has been passed down through hundreds of years and is now in the very nature of the gazelle – to be constantly on the watch for a predator, lurking around the bushes, behind the rocks and along the stream.

'Being afraid is the best gift the ancestors could have bequeathed to the gazelle – it shall keep her alive. However, being fast owing to these fears would also make her friendship with the earthworm difficult.

'Their pace would differ forever because the fears would differ forever. The lament of the innate incompatibility between the earthworm and the gazelle is futile.

'I am beautiful, said the gazelle to the earthworm. It was obvious that the reactions both evoked in others were quite different – and to make matters worse, both knew that. The earthworm knew it was creepy, slimy and almost disgusting to look at. Its skin was wrinkled, its colour was unappealing, and its movements were awkward. The gazelle knew she was delicate, stylish and beautiful. She evoked poems and sonnets.

'Beauty and constant adulation can cause vanity and it did in this case too. It can make you lose touch with things around you. The beautiful and the capable know it and assume it to be their birth right, for there is no better intoxication than knowing you are better and more beautiful than others. The more the gazelle spent time with the earthworm, the better she felt, for the contrast only accentuated her sense of superiority.

'Can you be selfless, like I am?' asked the earthworm to the gazelle. The gazelle did not quite understand. The earthworm knew all its life the drudgery of eating away and excreting the soil only made the soil richer. Life grows better where earthworms are aplenty. Even when they are not good to look at, they are useful. In that sense the earthworms are selfless – or at least infinitely more useful to others. Their life means something to others, even when others are blissfully unaware of the contributions made by them.

'It takes a large heart to be disliked, abhorred almost, treated with distaste and continue to do something that will make a difference to others' lives. It takes a large heart and the earthworm physically doesn't have one – perhaps that is why they are able to do it. Gazelle is busy in her vanity, consumed by her own beauty. She did not understand the question the earthworm had posed.

'What should we do together?' finally asked the earthworm. The gazelle replied – continue being who we are. I will keep strutting, and you keep crawling. I will keep being the beautiful one, you keep being the useful one. We both have a role today and rather important ones at that. *You will be crushed one day, and I will be hunted one day. The difference will hardly matter.'*

Having said that, Srinath just kept quiet – and then he said, 'The dying of the earthworm does matter, because he was useful before he was dead.'

He was not sure if his message reached the two gazelles in front of him. The two gazelles however understood it beyond doubt – that they had been slapped hard on their faces.

22. The Prison of Our Myths

The days of the extended lockdown were becoming intolerable, but not for the reason they had anticipated. The four guests in Hotel Landmark had realised that it was not the lockdown outside that was the cause of their agony – it was the realisation that they had been in a lockdown for all their lives. *There is no bigger grief for a human soul which has just discovered its bondage.*

The voice inside their minds had become a clamour by now. They had been sufficiently exposed in their own eyes. They had become aware that they were net takers from the universe – what they had taken far exceeded what they had given back. Even when they had given something, they had done so with an expectation of return – sometimes a favour, sometimes thankfulness and sometimes they had given just for the vanity of being known as a giver. There was no real giving.

They had become aware that their education, their knowledge, their capabilities were all tools to make them look good, look respectable, look better than others. There was always a one-upmanship with the world. They realised that they did not celebrate their goodness truly and deeply, because the intent had not been to enjoy, the intent always had been to prove.

They had realised that they were utterly incapable of greatness because deep inside them they were petty – there was no other way to say it – petty!

They realised finally that greatness comes when something larger than us appeals to us. *A life which cannot see beyond its own nose has simply no chance of creating something great.*

They realised that even animals live for themselves and care for their kin. There is no magic in being concerned about the wellbeing of your loved ones. Human lives acquire larger meaning when they mean something to even strangers, those we do not know, those who would not even know what good they are receiving from us and hence, will not be able to reciprocate with anything in return for that goodness. An act that comes despite that, is an act of greatness – and they realised that they had been incapable of greatness so far by that yardstick.

They became aware of their own narratives so far. They realised that they had told that narrative to themselves so many times that it had become a truth – a truth that was stale and that had stink coming out of it, and they had gotten used to that stink. They were no longer aware of it and hence it did not bother them.

They realised that all of us have a mythology about ourselves. Truth was hidden beneath the many layers of that mythology.

Our mythology suffers from all the abuses that classical myths suffer from – *one, it's always partial telling of the events of the past*, assuming that the events even happened, the details often become a casualty, because after a while no one remembers the facts, nor are facts available – only the myth survives.

Second and perhaps more diabolically – such *mythology is always designed to make us look better than we actually are!*

They realised that all of us like to weave a mythology about ourselves based on how things should be and not really how things are. We amplify our heroics however feeble they might be, and we clinically erase the evidence of our frailties. *Luckily, time is a great plastic surgeon.*

The myth building really begins to happen when the same story gets repeated again and again – the cementing is in the constant retelling – like the jaded party and get together jokes that get retold when school and college friends or even ex-colleages tell every time they meet. One notices the classical signs of mythology at work at such gatherings – all evidence of acrimony, deceit, pettiness, and envy and power struggle gets carefully sanitised – only the myth of laughter, innocence, bonhomie and undying friendships are upheld.

They realised that every person carries a million myths about themselves. The myth of uninterrupted and effortless success, the myth of a great professional, the myth of being a good companion, the myth of a good friend, the myth of a sacrificing and selfless adult who for others has given up on her ambitions, comforts and desires, and the most sinister myth of all – the myth of a victim, of how you were not at fault and how unfair everyone in the world has been to you.

They realised that they were constant creators, propagators and perpetuators of their own mythology. There are only two kinds of people on this — one who do not have finesse in mythology building and are noticed immediately for their uncouth and crude attempts; others who are artists, who do this with subtlety and sophistication. Both are frauds. The difference only is in the quality of the fraud.

They still did not know why they had done this all their lives – no one ever really knows it. They will one day realise that for most people, there is no choice but to create such mythologies. These myths that we weave help make our ordinary, mundane, mediocre and often pathetic existence a wee bit more tolerable. These mythologies help in drowning that nagging voice inside us which is trying to remind us of how hopelessly frail our egos have been, how temporary our successes have been, how meaningless our gloatings have been and how utterly forgettable our so-called victories have been.

The funny thing about all these rather unkind thoughts was that it was pulling them in two directions. At one level they were burdened by the realisation of their smallness. Yet on the other hand it was not a burden that was pulling them down. They were bubbling to do something about it. They did not know what or how, but the desire to make a difference had germinated.

Every time they met someone like Srinath Walke, that seed only gained a further momentum to break the shackles and sprout. The four were restless beyond measure – but it was a restlessness that wanted them to do something meaningful about it. Having recognised how uninspired their lives had been so far, they were ready to reimagine themselves. They wanted someone else to look back at them from the mirror – someone who stood for something bigger than what they had been so far.

It was under this tumult that Sunil Paswan returned that evening. They had not imagined the happiness they finally experienced in seeing him. It was as if family had returned.

The joy they experienced in seeing Sunil return, made it clear that Sunil Paswan was no longer merely a manager in the hotel they had been staying at. It was clear to them and more importantly it was clear to Sunil Paswan.

Sunil informed them of the tough time he went through. His wife had already been quarantined in the hospital much before he could meet her. He confirmed that there was nothing to worry and that she was well taken care of. He was more worried about them and had returned. He might have to go to visit her once in a while, but he could do that from here. In any case when he came to know that doctors and nurses fighting COVID were staying in his hotel, he could not stay home anymore. He knew he could play a role in fighting this scare by being the best hotel manager ever.

23. Liberation in Lockdown

In normal circumstances it is excruciatingly difficult for human beings to change even the smallest things about themselves. They are prisoners of their habits and rituals – of the time they get up, of the newspapers they read, of the breakfast they have, of the compulsiveness of all their daily rituals. Even the slightest change can leave them either mildly irritated or supremely agitated. A coffee drinker will refuse to drink tea, and should he be forced to do it, his mornings would be ruined. A change in newspaper will make the news unpalatable even when the news remains the same. Yet when it comes to situations which have even the slightest threat to life and limb, the change happens almost effortlessly. No habit is deep enough, no ritual is sacrosanct enough.

One of those days Sitam began the conversation. 'I have been thinking about our being stuck here for a long time. These new friends have made me question my life in unforeseen ways. Our lives will never be the same again.'

'In what ways?' asked Razia.

Sitam continued, 'At the simplest level it has the power for the *reimagination of the normal* – the normalcy of daily routines. Those of who us who were used to going to work and even those who are used to working at home, both have to reimagine and reorganise their day.

'The second level change it has the power to create, is the *reimagination of roles*. By the end of the lockdown almost everyone has flirted with doing new chores, if not completely done them. The cleaner, the cook, the guard, the home maker, the earner, are no longer someone else.'

Kulwant added, 'I think there is a third level of change it can also cause, the *reimagination of the notion of freedom* – particularly of the kind we had come to take for granted. Only a few would have experienced prolonged curfews – for a dominant majority it was the first experience. Freedom is just not a word anymore because everyone knows now how it feels when it is not there, when it is taken away. If just the absence of freedom of movement hurts so much, imagine how much the absence of freedom to think and speak would hurt.'

Sunil picked it up from there. 'Hopefully it will cause the *reimagination of priorities* too. Hopefully everyone will know what is really important and what is not. Hopefully we all will realise that relationships and health are far above the meaningless accumulation of things. I also pray that people will realise how significant those are who do the small things for us - the maids, the servants, the cleaners, the doctors, the nurses, the government servants, the constable, the traffic policemen; all of those are much bigger in their significance than we care to admit or respect.'

Manoj was oddly contemplative when he said, 'I wish that this will cause a *reimagination of reality* – of what is real and what is an illusion. I hope we will be able to make the distinction between what really matters and what doesn't – or at least we develop the perspicuity necessary to make that distinction. Hope we will be able to reimagine what is real success and real failure.'

'What is the likelihood that people would actually make any significant progress on any of these re-imaginations?' asked Sunil. He was pushing the envelope with much greater confidence ever since he had returned.

'Let me ask you all – I mean, how many of these re-imaginations have you managed to make so far or will be able to do once you go back?' he went in for the jugular.

If everyone at the table was shocked or hurt, they did not show it. They took Sunil's provocation in their stride. Perhaps it was the ultimate evidence that they were all friends now. *Friendship is when you allow the other to be ruthlessly honest with you – when you give the freedom to poke where it is tender, where it hurts.*

No one answered. Sunil did not push for an answer. Sometimes it is not important that a question is answered. The act of asking the question is powerful enough. The trouble with life often is not that answers are not available – it is often that the most profound questions have not been asked.

Questions must reach the deepest dungeons of the soul.

They all realised that there would be all kinds of people at the end – when it ends. They talked about all kinds.

Sunil talked about the first kind. 'The first ones would be *the hopeless*. These would be those who will come out at the other end precisely and exactly as they would have entered, and in all likelihood that is how they would remain for the rest of their lives. The solitude, the isolation, the change in rituals, the extended period of forced proximity with family and simultaneously prolonged period of distance from friends and work, the change of roles and even the availability of having long hours to contemplate, would create nothing – *zilch, nill, shunya.*

Some of us are utterly incapable of evolution. The most profound event in our lives would pass like a train passing through wilderness – creating a flutter for a while, after which everything settles down just like how it was before.

The second category was described by Manoj. 'These are the *non-converts.* They would go through this lockdown and the Corona crises like tourists. They will visit a place with curiosity, enjoy the sights and sounds and the new routine till it lasts but will return to their lives and go about living it exactly the way they always had.'

'How are they different from my category *sirjee*?' asked Sunil.

'Oh, they are different from them – your category did not experience anything; the new experience never reached their soul and hence they would not change. My category understood everything but refused to change – *they are much worse.*'

Sitam added his category, 'I think there will be a lot of *temporary converts.* These people who have learnt a bit of cooking, some levels of sharing of responsibility, discovered reading and the joys of exercise and have genuinely attempted to reimagine life. However, as things become normal, the realities of life will suck them in, and they will *resume everything that they had stopped and stop everything they had begun.*'

Razia commented, 'A close cousin of this type will be the *partial converts* – they are one notch better. They would not return from this crisis just as they were. They would continue with their new routine – their flirtations with health, sharing of responsibilities, teaching their kids, quality time with spouses, reading, listening to music, connecting with friends and family. However, they will fail to keep up with all such changes as life will resume.'

Kulwant described the last and the final category. 'These are *converts.* Full converts. They would reimagine their lives fully, completely and comprehensively. They will change their priorities on relationships, their emphasis on health, restore their connection with themselves, resume their passions, invest in their health and perhaps most importantly realise how *fickle life itself is and how great is the burden of our vanities.*'

Then, with a pause, Kulwant asked, *'Will there be such people…will we be such people?'*

∞

Sitam commented over dinner – 'I do not remember exactly where, but I read this poignant difference between a columnist and a novelist; a columnist writes for the day and most often what he writes for the day is part of the trash the next day, while a novelist writes with at least the intention of seeing his work outlast him.'

'And why is it that you remembered this now?' asked a visibly irritated Manoj.

Sitam continued as if he had not heard Manoj.

'In fact, many a time those remarkable novelists actually seem more and more relevant with each passing decade, sometimes acquiring cult status long after they are dead and gone.

'The column enjoys its fame every morning only to realise by noon that the fame is gone.

'A good novel is written when it finds resonance for the voice of many even if it is being written as the voice of one. A good novelist is adept at finding the echo of the collective even as she begins the search for her own voice.'

'So what is your point?' asked Manoj again.

'My point is – will we become trash tomorrow morning, or will we be remembered even a few years from now?' said the sombre Sitam.

'...and the question is, will we ever have the courage to look beyond our own limited lives and do something bigger and beyond it? Do our lives have any meaning whatsoever for anyone beyond those who matter to us? *I mean how miserably wretched this life is – only about me, only about us, only about ours?'*

It hit everyone hard. It was as if Sitam had articulated clearly what had been playing on their minds for the last couple of days.

The next few hours were perhaps the most powerful few hours of their lives. Sitam's comment had hit everyone very hard, shaking them from what appeared like a slumber that they had been in for their entire lives.

Everyone around them in Hotel Landmark was working for an ideal bigger than themselves, living in danger for others and in the process deriving some deeper meaning out of it.

No one is selfish by intent – but to live life for a higher ideal requires too much energy. Most do not have that energy and hence are condemned to live ordinary lives. They have talent, education and capability – but they do not have the energy to push themselves out of the orbit they are condemned to live in.

Then there are people like Srinath Walke who do not possess talent, education or any glorious capability. But he has the energy to push himself out of the orbit of selfish existence and work for something that is beyond himself, his immediate family and his personal ambitions.

The four guests kept on pouring their hearts out for many hours after dinner. They spoke of their pettiness, the smallness of their lives, the meaninglessness of their accomplishments and the hollowness of their desires.

In the same breath they spoke about how they were not the types who did great things. They spoke about never having opportunities or the burden of their responsibilities never allowing them space to do something big. They spoke about their limitations, their boundaries and their inabilities.

They felt stuck. They were oscillating between the inspiration of their desires and the yoke of their hesitations. They were mimicking the sordid saga of a million lives in these oscillations.

It appeared that they were waiting for greatness to knock on their doors, waiting for a miracle that would suddenly propel them from the depths of their ordinariness to the pinnacles of greatness.

They talked about how small they felt, how insignificant they found their possessions and accomplishments and what they would not sacrifice if only to live a few extra days of significance, meaning and greatness.

They blamed their responsibilities, the limitations of families, the pulls and pressures of their circumstances for their ordinariness.

It was a sorry state – the four of them. In that moment it was clear how little they understood the nature of greatness.

They did not understand that greatness is not an invitation that someone will ever extend, it's not a gift you will receive from someone, it's not a facility that will be provided, it is not a privilege that shall be bequeathed to you, it is not a lucky alignment of planets that will open doors for you.

Greatness is achieved by walking on very ordinary paths, by doing very mundane tasks, by dealing with the dirty and diseased, by thinking of others even when there is compulsive temptation to think about yourself. *Greatness never reveals itself as greatness.*

'Are you all serious about what you have been talking?' asked Sunil, in a voice which was both stern and commanding. '...are you serious about making a difference?'

Everyone looked at Sunil expectantly. In the next few minutes Sunil laid out the plan that would not only shake them to their core but also lay the foundation of a new life. The great Sunil Paswan from the district Ara of Bihar.

'Let us all go and work as volunteers in the hospital that these doctors and nurses work. In any case you all have nothing to do but remain stuck here. I will find out what best each one of you can do there to contribute. I will arrange for passes and get permissions.

Sunil dropped his suggestion like a bomb. Everyone knew about the risks associated with the choice. They were aware of the people back home who needed to be informed. They knew that they had not done anything remotely like this in their entire lives. They knew in their hearts they will be called insane when word will spread. They were all thinking of dozens of reasons why this was an extremely bad and dangerous idea.

Yet there was this little voice in their ears which was screaming, 'THIS IS YOUR ONLY CHANCE!'

PART 2

Sunil Paswan had indeed dropped a bomb shell by his suggestion, alarming in its boldness and deep in its implications, but the good thing about it this time was that they were ready. Their souls were ready!

Even the most profound inspiration around us can just caress us and move on, leaving us untouched for all practical purposes if we are not ready.

All our lives we wait for something or someone to trigger our sense of a grand design for life, that existential ache that all human beings are born with, that would propel us to do something that will leave an imprint, that will create something that will outlive us. Many cannot articulate this need, but all have it. Most do not understand that ache, only a few can describe it, and hence even fewer do something about it.

The reason why most of us live ordinary lives is not because there is no inspiration that will ignite us to such an act, but because we are not ready to receive the gift. This time, those four in Hotel Landmark, were ready.

It had taken a month of lockdown, long hours of solitude, intermittent conflicts, and finally the gradual revelation of their own pettiness, that had made them ready and willing to accept the challenge Sunil Paswan had thrown at them.

The lockdown had managed to liberate them. It became clear to each one of them that salvation was a fraud perpetuated by those who promise it but could never deliver it. We must chase liberation, not only because it is achievable but also because we do not need anyone else to deliver it for us.

The next few days were crazy. Sunil was on the job. He had promised them liberation and he was keen to deliver it. He was constantly on the phone, talking, finding, pulling strings, asking for favours. It took him four days of extraordinary jugaad to arrange an opportunity to redeem them from the petty lives they had been living.

He found a nearby government hospital, which agreed to take them as volunteers, where all of them could participate in fighting the biggest human crises that the world had ever seen. The hospital had been converted into a nodal Covid treatment centre in that area.

They chose to play roles that they wanted, and they could – basking in the satisfaction that when this will all be over, they would not have watched it from the margins.

Sitam would work as the co-coordinator in the nursing department, overseeing the massive deployment of the thin nursing staff. His soul would experience pride.

Razia would be working with the doctors to manage their duty rosters. She would experience the life of her husband, but this time through very different eyes, and to very different outcomes – and more than anything else, at the end of it she would start respecting Srijith and his choices. Her soul would experience meaningfulness.

Kulwant took on the role of taking care of the families who accompanied the patients. In a crisis like this, families were at equal risk and would go through tremendous fear given the overall atmosphere of uncertainty – someone had to take care of them too. Someone like Kulwant, who knew what pain was, what grief was, someone who had seen enough of life not to be surprised by the presence of pain and its diabolic outcomes, was best placed to do so. Her soul would experience bliss.

Manoj would be working with the paramedics, the support staff. He would be interacting with the cleaners, the ward boys – the last havaldars in this fight. Interestingly, he chose this role himself. He was sick and tired of his notions of privilege, the hollowness of the people he thought were good enough for him and his own hollowness in believing in this definition of elitism. He wanted penance. His soul would get penance.

Sunil Paswan took the job of dealing with the incoming patients. He would stand right outside the door, receiving families and guiding them through the steps required to deal with the treatment process. In a lot of ways, he was the doorman again. He had chosen to go back to do exactly the role he thought he had progressed from. His soul would be at home finally.

24. Sitam: Some Burdens are a Relief

Sitam witnessed the working conditions of the nurses in the hospital and what he saw shocked him to his bones. He had known all this while that the nurses existed as an important pillar of a hospital infrastructure — those young girls and women who would be silently moving across the corridors carrying trays and medicines, with calm and composure on their faces despite being in the middle of brazen morbidity.

He had known of them but never really known them, and perhaps that is why what he discovered, shook him so badly. More than the conditions of the nurses, his own ignorance hit him hard. He could not digest his distance from reality as ignorance – he knew it was insensitivity.

It is not our ignorance that makes us feel bad, it's the realisation that we allowed such an ignorance to exist in the first place that hits us harder.

He saw the nurses working two shifts back to back with no rest and respite – and then come back to work within a few hours just because a colleague would have called sick. They would do that with a smile. They would sleep in any corner that they could find, rarely having the luxury of lying down. They would hunch on files, on their arms, against a door or a wall, or wherever they got a moment of support.

They knew that every minute of rest when they could comfort their weary eyes was vital to keep them fresh, so that then they would have the energy to have a look at the next patient with attentiveness and concentration.

They had to be fresh and alert each time they looked at a patient and yet their own bodies would be worn out, their limbs would be aching, and their energy would have been sucked out of every sinew.

He would sometimes enter cramped nursing stations and see two or three of them practically dozing off on each other. The hospital was not designed for the comfort of its nurses, for their rest – and the nurses would not have the moral courage to take rest in plain sight of the patients; their high sense of duty did not allow them to do so.

Sitam felt guilty about his job and its privileges. He felt a deep-seated anger with himself – for all the times he had hated his job and called it boring, dissatisfying and meaningless. He felt miserable about all the times he had called his job stressful. He felt guilty of his privileged place in the warm bosom of the Indian bureaucracy, secure in knowing that no one was watching, happy in knowing that even if he screwed up, nothing would happen. The Indian state will back him and clean his mess.

He also looked back at his job in the food and supplies distribution within the Indian bureaucracy and felt a deep surge of disgust at himself – for all the disdain he had for his fortunes. The world outside regarded him as elite, for he had cracked the UPSC and was a senior bureaucrat. In his eyes since he was not of an IAS or IPS cadre his job was not good enough for him. He had never felt any semblance of pride in his job. He looked at the nurses and he was reminded of his folly. There is respite for those whose profession and successes are considered of lesser significance by others; there is no liberation for those who in their own hearts do not own any pride in their professions and successes. They live condemned lives.

He saw the treatment these nurses had to swallow every hour. They were the second-class citizens in the nation of health professionals. The doctors treated them like appendages. They would be shouted upon, or taken for granted, or just not acknowledged for the jobs that they did, or the immense value they brought to the process of healing in the hospitals.

Even when they would not be pulled up, the vibes were enough to remind them of their place in the hierarchy of things. Those vibes put them into their slots, clearly many levels lower than the doctor.

It is a miracle to be inspired under such a working set up, where not only are you clear about your subservient status, but also given a daily reminder of it. Yet the nurses were a living testimony of inspired lives.

No one realises that after the doctor is long gone, it is the nurses who remain behind, tending to the body which is diseased and a mind which is in turmoil. The irony was that when the patient recovered, he also remembers to thank the doctor but usually forgets the nurse. The discrimination was inbuilt into the psyche of the system.

'It is only a miracle that we have so many nurses still coming to work every day, willing to give their tenderness and warmth to an ungrateful system,' thought Sitam to himself, more out of self-loathing than anything else.

Sitam would see the nurses tending the Covid patients apart from the non-Covid ones and wondered if they were ever scared. He remembered his days in the lockdown and how afraid they all were.

Sitam learnt so many things about the nurses, some of which emerged from the conversations he had with them and some by sheer observations. It was obvious they were overworked and underpaid. It was also clear that their convenience came much after that of the doctors. What he could not fathom was their source of commitment, which despite such demanding circumstances still made them show up and show up smiling.

He wanted to enter the souls of nurses to know more about the fountain of their inspiration.

He also became aware of another human travesty – how easily and loosely we use the word inspiration and how little do we understand it.

Sitam remained at this job over the coming few months. He would receive calls from his wife who would urge him to return home. She could not understand why he was taking all this risk. She even called him a fool, which he took as a validation of sorts.

He tried his level best to explain his reasons for doing this and he came to a new realisation about relationships.

Even in the closest of relationships it is impossible to explain why we do what we do, why it is important for us to do certain things, why we need to have certain things. It is during these moments, when you cannot explain such things to even close companions, spouse and parents, that you realise that ultimately all of us will remain un-understood all our lives. There will be a part of us that no one else will ever understand completely.

Some of us will make peace with that trauma, most will make it a life-long angst, and only the rare will realise that it is the nature of life. *All of us must carry the cross of not being understood.*

Despite the regular prodding, Sitam could not make himself leave. Every now and then he would wonder about his reasons of being here, despite the freedom to leave any moment.

There was no force, no duty, no job compulsion that was keeping him here. There was no obligation, no pressure, no moral compunction that was holding him back. The only thing that was holding him back was a desperate need to do something bigger than his own wretched needs and desires. He wanted to feel special and he realised that all these years he was seeking that fulfilment through means that were incomplete, ineffective and hollow.

He realised that spending time here in this hospital, playing a small but meaningful role in a larger cause, in lending a helping hand to the nurses to do their jobs well, he was getting what he never had so far – *joy*.

He was sleeping well these days. Without the Old Monk.

One night in the hotel, Sitam shared with his friends, 'Every life has a burden.'

Manoj asked – 'Meaning?'

He continued, 'Burden not in the sense that we understand the word generally – as a heavy cross around the neck, a yoke of the soul that is so heavy that it chokes movement, but burden in the sense of a grand purpose of the life's being.

'The artist's burden is to express. The painter's burden is to bring the canvas alive with his joy and his grief, his memories and his interpretations. The poet's and the writer's burden is to weave tales with words. The social worker's burden is community good. The businessman's burden is profit and wealth creation. The home maker's burden is a happy home. The film maker's burden is to tell an engaging story. Each one of us has a destined burden – that only we know and that only we shall discover – if we are lucky.

'Such a burden gives direction. It gives reason to act, continue and stretch our limits – more importantly, it gives meaning to everything. The burden does not let us be in peace till it is listened to, attended to and nourished. It *demands* that we nurse it. It just won't let us be! Even when all else is taken care of, an unattended burden can make life look unbearable – and when it is well - tended to, it makes the soul sing.

'Most do not know their burden yet and so live like zombies, in a state of hangover where senses are dull, faculties are dim, and awareness is poor. It's like flipping the pages of a book without a purpose – scanning through the lines creates only an illusion of reading but never really communicates the meaning embedded in it. A life without a burden is worthy of sympathy if not pity.

'You know, when I spend time with the nurses, I feel that I am finally blessed to have a burden. Life without this burden was...well, such a monstrous burden.

Sitam smiled despite the sombre mood. So did everyone else.

In that moment they knew, Sitam had been liberated.

25. Razia is Ganga

Razia was married to a doctor. She was aware of the lives doctors lived, or so she thought. She had seen Srijith coming home weary and tired from long hours in the government hospital, most days.

'It is a job, maybe a tad tougher one,' she had told herself. It was only now she came to see up close what that job really entailed. She saw the profession of doctors in an absolutely new light. Every day she spent in that hospital, apart from changing her opinion about doctors would make her fall deeper and deeper in love with Srijith.

Love does not have a core, or a centre, from where its magic and its power emanate. Most of us do not get this and we keep searching its innermost core, as if there is a magical stone lying at the centre; finding which will solve its mysteries. It is not a treasure hunt leading to that core. Love only has layers – one below the next. Understanding love is just peeling one layer after the next and rejoicing the act of that discovery. By the time love starts to make sense to us, it can no longer be reduced to any one emotion; it is the sum total of all the layers discovered so far. Those who do not get these layers, in a lot of way, do not get the nature of love itself. As long as two people can keep peeling those layers and keep the joys of that discovery alive, they keep the love between them alive. The day there are no more layers left, love begins to atrophy.

Razia was attracted to Srijith when they met, much later she found a friendship in her love for him. Now Razia had discovered the next layer of that love – *respect.*

She also reached another conclusion – that the difference of professions between a husband and wife has much to do with the longevity and survival of marriages. She remembered her conversations with friends. A common refrain by everyone was about how certain parts of their marriages were getting unhinged, which could be linked to peculiarity of the profession of their spouses. Late hours in travel-related jobs, unpredictability of fortunes in sales-related jobs, absent mindedness in creative jobs – and for Razia, it was the problem of receiving an absolutely emotionally drained husband at the end of each day.

Srijith would reach back home as a body robbed of appetite for food and conversation. She would be irritated with him for his utter lack of attention to anything at home and more importantly to her. She would expect companionship, warmth and its expression; Srijith would have no energy to demonstrate any of that. After a while she started to doubt everything about love, as is doubted by most who have loved and gone through the moderating effects of converting it into a marriage. As she spent more time with the doctors here, she realised that none of that was Srijith's fault.

Every profession gives something to the practitioner – but every profession also kills you in many ways. Most professions ruin marriages in unspoken ways. In fact, amongst all the reasons why marriages fail, the contribution of the professions of the spouses attracts the least attention. Each profession exacts a price. Most explain it away as a price you pay for belonging to that profession. Most do not have the intelligence to know the price they have paid in choosing their vocations and very few have the freedom to blame it.

With every passing day in the hospital, interacting with the doctors, Razia realised that it was a miracle that Srijith could give her the time and attention that he managed to give. Most doctors reach home so deadened they can only sleep, forget expressing love.

She saw doctors in that hospital at the forefront of the fight against the greatest threat that humanity had faced in a century or so. They did so under tremendously adverse circumstances. The hospital was brimming beyond capacity. A 250-bed hospital had 500 plus patients. Patients were crammed together and those waiting for their turn were lying in the corridors. Medicines were scarce and so were ventilators.

In any case no one quite knew what would work. It was a game of patience and chance, waiting to see how the patient would respond to the virus. Some were lucky to show little symptoms and others struggled to breathe.

It is trauma to see a person struggling to breathe. We take the act of breathing for granted, but the sight of a patient in a fit of cough, echoing a wheezing sound of laboured breath, can shake the strongest of us. The sound of that breath is a desperate sound, trying its level best to hold on to life. The screech emerging from the lungs is a call for help.

In the hospital Razia realised that death was in the corners, but the fear of death was everywhere. It made the air even heavier. More than the virus it was this fear which made breathing impossible. If the virus was making breathing difficult for those who were infected, it made breathing impossible for everyone else.

The healthy had an additional burden of giving hope too. In such a place where even the greatest optimist would lose his will to stay in the fight, the doctors had to not only cure, but also give hope.

Razia realised it was criminal to expect a normal life from a human being who has to witness such sights of disease and decay for the whole day. How would a person who has witnessed the fragility of human life from such close quarters, proclaim eternal love?

Those who have seen too much life and too much death lose faith not only in love, the institution of love, but in the very concept of it.

When the next moment of life hinges on the cruel hands of fate and an even more cruel game of chance, one wonders if such a thing called love even exists? Are we not fools to believe in it and even worse, expect it?

She also realised there was something worse than that too – that in a relationship, one person would reach the stage of questioning the very notion of love and its impossibility, and the other person would still be a romantic, who would make love and the pursuit of love as the core pursuit of life. It was a cruel combination.

She realised her marriage, despite everything that was working so beautifully, was at risk of this cruelty. The more she worked in this hospital the more she became aware of it.

Her mind went back to the plight of the doctors. They were struggling to feel safe. In the initial days they struggled to get the right protective gear. Some complained of the harsh material, others of rashes and excessive sweating. It was claustrophobic wearing them and agonising to move around in them. They could not change during the day, could not go to relieve themselves and in most cases could not breathe comfortably.

Razia wondered what these doctors felt about hope. She wondered if they were fearful of their own lives. She wondered how they were able to perform their own duties battling their own demons. The doctors still cracked jokes and enjoyed a light moment amongst themselves and it appeared to her that they had a protective layer not only on their bodies but also on their souls. Neither the virus could enter, nor its fear.

In the evenings the four of them would meet once in a while. Each one had a different schedule. One of those evenings Razia began a monologue. She spoke and spoke to all, but in effect she spoke to herself. She spoke about the river Ganga, but everyone knew that she was speaking about herself.

'I wonder sometimes what Ganga feels while it springs from Bhagirathi, and hurtles down the mountains with youthful vigour, untamed and flirting with her constraints. I wonder if she is even aware of her destiny and the fact that the mountains Maybe the place where she took birth but her end will come some 2000 miles away in faraway unknown land, away from the surroundings that she knows as home.

'I wonder what she feels when the incline vanishes, and she assumes the calm of the plains. I wonder what goes through her soul at Haridwar where she experiences the tapering of her vigour, and the forced demands on her composure. I wonder if she is mentally even prepared for the long arduous calm that lies ahead.

'I wonder if she is bored as she travels through the plains haunted by the memory of the earlier avatar, and experiences angst for that life. I wonder if she misses her wayward ways, the swing of her hips, the hope in her meander. I wonder if she questions the supreme confidence that she had about herself and her ability to chart her own course.

'I wonder whether she even knows as she crosses into Bengal that she is now at the beginning of her last leg. Is she satisfied with the way things have turned out or does she have regrets?

'I wonder if she remembers the banks she has crossed; are they etched in her memory, will she be able to recollect those villages, hamlets and cities effortlessly or will she struggle to trace a smile here and a tear there?

'I wonder, what if Ganga were to know that no one else remembers her much accept the fact they are accustomed to her presence, and I wonder what the banks would feel if Ganga has only a hazy recollection of them.

'I wonder if Ganga ever wants to trace her journey back, to relive her journey and if that chance is given, would she do it in exactly the same way or will she change the course and character of her odyssey?'

'I wish Ganga could talk to me and let me know her heart.'

Kulwant put her hand over Razia's head like a mother would do and said – 'You have all the answers Razia. You do not have to wonder about Ganga anymore.'

Razia smiled warmly.

In that moment they knew Razia had been liberated.

26. Kulwant – Validation-free

The country and the world went through its own awakening in the coming days. The pandemic spared no one. The numbers kept multiplying without caring for their masters. Daily infection rates in one state became what the national figures were until recently. Safe zones became red zones and red zones started to report fatalities. Countries which thought they had won over the tiny virus reported a resurgence. Those who always imagined their lives to be safe and above the mundane concerns of the *hoi-polloi,* were shocked to find themselves as susceptible to the virus as anyone else. In a lot of ways, the world truly became equal and flat this time – perhaps for the first time. No one noticed the philosophical implications of this as they were busy fighting the virus. *Life often offers us deep philosophical lessons, but we are too busy.*

The variety of responses was comical. On the one hand the best of human attributes were on full display – people were coming out in large numbers to contribute, donate, and help. On the other hand, the deepest divisions amongst people were also magnified. Every time a case would be detected in posh colonies and condominiums, the maids would be stopped entries. Swarms of migrants returned to their villages, disgorged from the cities they had built on the sweat of their brow and the strength of their muscles. Now, in the moment of absolute duress, they had been abandoned. They walked, cycled and hitched back to the comfort of their native villages.

Kulwant would often wonder if the returning labourers would be welcomed back in their villages with open hearts. Here were those, who had abandoned their villages when it suited them and now when they were rejected by their new homes, they were returning – and this time with a distinct possibility of being carriers of a danger that the villages they were returning to, were unequipped to handle.

The contours of prodigals returning are complex and impossible to ascertain from a distance. Each home would have been a theatre of this complex human drama and each household would be shouldering the burden of that drama in its unique ways.

New words became a part of everyday usage. Asymptomatic was one of them. There was almost a caste system in those who were infected. The worst were those who demonstrated the worst of Covid symptoms. The asymptomatic were let off easily. The truth was that the asymptomatic wwere the most dangerous – because they would consider themselves as relatively safe and hence were more prone to display a behaviour that would put others at risk. They were the silent carriers.

Kulwant smiled when she realised how similar this was to her understanding of human frailties. The worst, without an exception are the asymptomatic carriers. There are those amongst us who display envy, greed, anger, biases, vileness and pettiness. They are easy to spot and hence easy to deal with. However, many more carry these frailties deep in their hearts, carefully concealed, but not controlled – they are more dangerous.

Mumbai and all other cities reopened in fits and bursts. It went through alternate cycles of hope and despair. The numbers screamed in the news every morning about those infected and died. Kulwant wanted to tell the news channels to stop sharing these numbers – it was only amplifying the mood of despair.

Kulwant noticed something else that she kept on musing over for a long time – 'How can a place smell of despair and hope at the same time?'

Every day spent in this hospital bore witness to the simultaneous play of hope and despair – a heady concoction of soul crushing fear and sombre reassurances. In her rather long life, Kulwant was familiar with death and decay. She had seen lives withering away. However, morbidity at this scale bore a hole in her heart, but at the same time also helped in springing the fountain of humility in her.

The eventuality of our end can be numbing. It is a road that has no U-turn; a river flows only in one direction.

She realised that in a way everyday living is a carefully constructed denial of this eventuality. We populate all our time with so much activity so that it can act as a sophisticated charade to make us forget that we are actually hurtling towards our end. Witnessing death and sickness puts things in perspective.

She also saw amidst the smell of despair, people who were the embodiment of hope. Everyone who came here was in search of assurance. Everyone wants to hear that they have somehow slowed down their end. They have anguish in their eyes, meekness, vulnerability, and a scare that is screaming through their gaze. Even when they know the truth, it cannot be uttered, for nothing kills a man faster than the death of hope.

She tried very hard but could not fathom the minds of those who worked at the hospital – the young nurses and ward boys; the emergency ward Junior doctors, the residents – the terribly overworked, under-slept and mostly underpaid staff. Who would choose out of their own volition, a profession which has misery, pain, grief, agony and despair as companions for daily living?

Kulwant was taking care of the family members who were in the hospital because their loved ones were undergoing treatment. They were largely covid patients, although there were others too. She would comfort them, counsel them and above all else give them hope. *'Sab theek ho jayega'* is worth more than many antibiotics!

Kulwant understood many things about sickness. She realised that sickness is experienced by the entire family and death perhaps by an entire community. The family members who accompany the sick to the hospital suffer as much or even more than the patient. The sick goes through pain, but the family goes through anguish.

Accompanying a Covid patient was even more profound because it tested the strength of family ties like never before. It had been almost a generation, after the times of tuberculosis and leprosy, that families were dealing with something contagious, something that their loved ones had the possibility of passing on to them. This was a new fear. It was difficult to deal with love and fear simultaneously. Love demanded of them to accompany family to the hospital; fear kept them worrying.

Kulwant realised that the patient may depend only on medicines to get better, but families needed much more. They needed hope and comfort – unfortunately hospitals were ill-equipped to offer both. Doctors and nurses were too busy dealing with the act of treatment. Their priority was the patient, not the families.

Kulwant also realised that the patients usually looked for the signs of their conditions not on the face of the doctor or the nurses, but in the eyes of family members. Those eyes would never betray the truth. One look in the eyes of a mother or a wife would tell a patient if he is recovering or the chances of survival are grim. She was solving that look.

In the course of supporting the families, Kulwant also came to the realisation that she had played that role all these years – first for the husband and then for her children.

A housewife is a strange vocation. If chosen voluntarily, it is rewarding; it is burdensome for those upon whom it is thrust. The worst part of it is not that it is a prison one never comes out from, the worst part of it is that it is systemically glamorized. The worst part of it is that its virtues are eulogised, and its horrors often brushed under the carpet. The worst are those who have grown up during the times when they did not know any better but have survived long enough to know that their lives could have meant much more. The worst violence against another human being is the stifling of their potential.

Kulwant looked back at her life and realised it had been all about someone else creating a charter of her responsibilities, as defined by the norms of the society that she was accidentally born into. She had no choice in accepting those norms or questioning their logic or validity. The sheer thanklessness towards career housewives that is ingrained in everyone around her, her husband and son even, angered her. She wanted to shake them up and remind them of her role in their success.

So far, she had been anguished at not being acknowledged sufficiently for that role, but with each passing day in the hospital she realised, she did not need that acknowledgement. She realised only she was the custodian of her self-worth; that no one else was responsible for determining it. She realised that all these years she was looking for a validation that was never needed.

Kulwant was relieved of the burden she had carried all these years, the pursuit of seeking someone else to confirm that she had done a good job of being a wife and a mother. She no longer felt any need for it.

A soul no longer needing validation from another human being is freer than a bird.

27. Manoj – Reimagining Superiority

He was the bird. He was the bird in the dream.

The birds in the next nest woke him. He was unaware of the whispers of an about-to-be lit morning sky. Like most, he rarely witnessed early mornings, and even when he did, he was too engrossed in the previous day's experience to soak in its pristine solace.

One must look at the skies changing their moods during early mornings. The darkness pixilates into hues of grey as the sky bares itself, almost disrobing in slow motion. One is not prepared for everything to become suddenly clear, but it does. It is like we were understanding life – one moment it's a mystery and then the meaning unveils itself, and finally with the snap of a finger, it is all clear.

He did not know much about life, but this much he had grudgingly come to realise – understanding it was the easy part; accepting it was tricky. All of us are prisoners of something or someone. He had to put aside such philosophising because he had to deal with the onerous task of getting up and getting ready to fly. Flying high is a full-time job, an obsession. There is no independence from it for those who are habituated to it. Flying high is addictive.

He realised that everyone leaves behind something at the nest as he steps out in the morning for the day's flight, and having spent the whole day outside, comes back a little more incomplete every evening, a little more depleted.

He also remembered older birds mumbling something about their search for completeness. He had never understood them and why that search was so difficult for them – it was easy and effortless to him.

The older birds would mumble so much mumbo jumbo that his head would spin. They would talk about how every adult is incomplete in a peculiar way and because of peculiar circumstances. They would talk about how every adult is drunk on the mistaken pride of his uniqueness and brilliance, strength and his ability to move the world.

'We are withering away daily,' he heard another bird sing. 'There is no running away from this – that time is short. Those who don't have a destination suffer from it, those who have a destination but no plan suffer from it, and those who have everything but have no flight in their wings suffer from it.'

Yet another bird was telling him her story, 'I was once in an iron cage. I had felt miserable in it. Every cage has a peculiar curse – it torments in a specific way. Some have lack of space, some are not airy enough, some have iron bars, and in some cases, there is nothing to see beyond those bars – but above all, the worse thing about all cages is, Captivity. Captivity is the mother of all curses. I had fought my way out of that cage and flown away to freedom. However, I carried that cage in my mind. In many ways I am still in that cage because I think of it so often. There is no independence from the cages we were once thrust into.' Said the bird finally.

Manoj woke up with a start from this dream one morning and wondered who that bird was and what was the import of those stories on him. He wondered if the dream was trying to tell him something. He got ready and went to the hospital.

Manoj had chosen to be with the front-line workers in the hospital. It was in the spur of a moment that he had taken this decision – he had never felt more right in taking a decision in his entire life.

He was a strange companion to the toilet cleaner, the ward boy, and the attendant who changed blood-stained sheets.

Manoj Joshi, the Enginner-MBA high-flying elite, the best the current education infrastructure could produce, with an ego the size of a giant volcano, a self-view which was inflated beyond logical proportions, with the airs of a modern day emperor, one who would consider the colleges people have gone to before deciding the merit of their arguments, was now rubbing shoulders with the lowest rung of this hospital – and happily so!

All his life he had floated above everyone else, smug in the belief of his superiority, linked to education, expertise, and sophistication. He was convinced of his superiority all his life. With every passing day in this hospital and in interacting with the people he was working with, that sense of superiority was fraying at its edges – not because the confidence itself was misplaced, but because he was coming to the conclusion that such superiority, even if true, is transient at best.

He was undergoing a new experience and in some ways was being chiselled into a new person with that experience.

One of the ways in which we can save ourselves from the tendency to take ourselves too seriously, is to have friends who are very different from us, belonging to very different professions and preferably who are less endowed than us.

Manoj experienced calm in his daily interactions with his new friends. He was mesmerised by how little it took them to be happy. He figured out how easy it was for them to deal with the stress that came with their jobs and this shocked him. He was blown away by their fortitude and became aware of his own fears.

He ate with them, took a drag of the humble bidi with them, and listened to the stories of their families – a young child they had not seen for weeks, ailing parents back in the villages, teenage children who were not ready to identify with their ways of living or the values they practiced.

He would keep thinking about the absolute calm on the faces of these workers, despite where they would have just returned from – some would have returned from an operation theatre watching someone take his last breath, some would have returned from the ICU where a terminally ill patient would be lying like a vegetable, some would have just watched the wailing around a dead body, some would have returned from the COVID ward watching, the sombre look on every face that had death written all over.

Yet when they met him, they met him with so much excitement and so much affection that Manoj would feel guilty. Everyone could feel proud that Manoj was talking to them and interacting with them. They wanted nothing from him – just his company. Such purity made Manoj purer. The authenticity rubbed on him. He began to desire similar simplicity in his life, a similar lightness of the soul. He started to desire something that he never thought he would desire.

Manoj was the most liberated of the erstwhile guests of Hotel Landmark.

All his life Manoj was convinced of his philosophies in life. He was convinced of his devil-may-care attitude towards fellow human beings in the pursuit of his ambitions. He was convinced about the constraints human emotions put on the wheels of progress. He was convinced that career growth and material accomplishments were the only credible ways to measure success. He was convinced that victory explains everything, and power makes us sleep warm. However, he was no longer sure about anything anymore. He had begun harbouring doubts on all his long-held beliefs. *True growth is always in reaching the point where what we always thought of as truth becomes worth questioning.*

There was one realisation that stood head and shoulders above everything else that he had held as his truth so far. So far, he had never entertained the thought of his own mortality. It had never occurred to him that he could die. He knew of death as someone else's guest but had never imagined that she could knock on his doors also. He finally entertained that thought. He became acutely aware that he could die.

The realisation triggered a thousand unfamiliar thoughts in him. He thought of how he will be remembered – will he be loved, feared or admired? Will people regret his passing away or rejoice or worst still, would they give a damn? Will there be people who will miss him? Will his life mean something to someone, where it will be said of him – 'I owe this to Manoj'. He saw the ordinary dying and he saw the powerful dying with as little fuss as anyone else. He saw mighty businessmen dying of a tiny virus and the politician who spent his entire life controlling others, not being able to control his bowels. He saw the significant dying, he saw the beautiful dying, he saw the vain dying. He experienced the inescapability of death.

In the agony of the place he also thought of his career and was surprised with his thoughts. He questioned the manner of his dealing with people, his high handedness, his need for absolute control and his unwillingness to be questioned. He realised that institutions are a lot like life – they move on. After a few years they do not remember anyone. New emperors replace the old ones, who again repeat the vanity of irreplaceability.

He was not surprised with the questions per se, because these questions were not new – what was new to him was that he was bothered by these questions. He had never imagined they would. It was becoming more and more important to him to know the answers to these questions, to settle them in his mind. He used to hate such questions earlier, often looking at them with disdain; now he was enjoying these questions and his struggle to seek answers to them.

In interacting with those who were less endowed and less educated than him, and after spending time with those who were lesser than him in every conceivable way he had so far compared human beings – and finally arriving at the conclusion that it was he who was lesser than them, Manoj experienced a peace that he never knew existed.

Manoj experienced liberation in that peace.

28. Sunil Paswan – What you run away from, runs with you

When bad news hits human beings, they usually begin with disbelief, often attributing it to their favourite scapegoats. Each of us have pet scapegoats who shoulder the burden of all our misfortunes. It can be karma, it can be conspiracy of the neighbour or the colleague, the general political nature of man, his deplorable morals and if nothing else, then destiny. Destiny is a broad term, which has the power to explain away all our misfortunes – even those which have been created by our own follies and foolishness. It takes a while before the eventuality of bad news is budgeted in the rhythm and routine of our lives. Covid was like that.

Right up until the end of April the world behaved as if this was a bad dream that will go away. It was only towards the end of the month that it started to dawn upon man and his institutions that the world had been turned upside down. The month of May witnessed tentative attempts to deal with the changes that Covid was demanding of individuals, families and institutions – all of whom were singularly unprepared to make that transition.

The four guests of Hotel Landmark were back in the comfort of their homes and loved ones by the end of July, except one – Sunil Paswan. He continued his work as the unofficial doorman of the hospital right up until his last day, in the hospital as well as on this earth, the 15th of August, when like his nation decades ago, he was liberated from what he had run away from, 30 years ago from his village in the district Ara in Bihar.

During one of those days as the doorman in the hospital, Sunil thought about fishes – the fishes that swim together, that swam together, from the head of the river to the mouth of the sea.

He realised that the fishes start as a tight knit school, but each of them have a unique journey, as it would eventually dawn on them much later.

He realised that young fishes jostle with enthusiasm and an overt display of competitiveness. The competition may not necessarily be to achieve something, but many a time, only for the sake of it – and even this would eventually dawn on them only many years later. The jostle of the early years is just a jostle for space, a jostle for being seen and heard, a jostle to make their presence felt, a jostle to overcome the fear of being left out, of being a nobody. *Nobody wants to be a nobody.*

The jostle between the fishes, even if they are all travelling together towards the same destination, and even if the river is big enough for everyone, gives a sense of importance – even though they know that *they are up against the river and not up against each other.*

Sunil realised that fishes are a nervous lot. They disperse at the hint of danger even when they travel together. The moment they sense fear they leave the school and fend for themselves. So, they learn a lesson that becomes their cross to carry thereafter – they now know that when it comes to matters of life and death, they are alone. In the purest sense, they are never of the school anymore, for the school anymore and with the school anymore. They are individuals who are just travelling together but alone. The river looms over them; its vagaries take over; idealism and camaraderie becomes innocent casualities. This should not be – but the river is inescapable. *The rivers we all travel are inescapable.*

Sunil thought of the river's tide and how it is a nightmare for the fish. It is uneven, unpredictable and full of tantrums. The river also has to live up to its reputation. Its water must surprise, its flow must shock, and its meander must evoke incredulity. In delivering the surprise, shock and incredulity the river is being the river. The fish has no business to complain, fret and fume. The fish has only one business – to swim. Swim forward. Dodge deftly but swim forward. Make a delicate dive or a bold manoeuvre or make a radical about turn, but eventually swim forward. The tango between the river and fish must continue. It's a dance – it's a romance in a lot of ways.

Sunil had an epiphany about fishes – Fishes swim for most part of their lives. Some swim better than others. Some faster than others, some dive better, some turn better, some dodge better, some longer than others. Each one has swim in their fins, some better in this way and some better in another way. As they begin their journey at the mouth of the river, there is a distinct tendency to show off what they could do better and hide what they could not. The vanity of abilities is in full display and everyone is culpable. One must not hold it against the fishes though – vanity is the opium of the youth. It keeps them going – for a while. It won't keep them swimming forever, something they do not know now but they will, eventually.

Everyone in the school of fishes would hold a regret. Some would regret having done something, some of having not done something, some of taking things easy and some taking things too seriously, some of being misused in relationships and some of not having forged any relationships. It would just not matter eventually as they would discover many years later.

Sunil Paswan, the man from Ara, finally concluded this about fishes and through his conclusion about fishes, concluded this about himself, people and life – that all the fishes that had begun at the mouth of the river may not reach the ocean, but they travel what is due to them. Some stop on the way, some reach the end of the journey and flow into the ocean. There is no way to find out what is a better fate – reaching the ocean or remaining in the river. It does not matter at all. Many years later the only thing that they would rejoice and be thankful about is the camaraderie that gets forged by swimming in the same river at the same time – of swimming together.

Sunil took the job of receiving families at the doors of the hospital when patients and their families would disgorge from all kinds of vehicles, but with one common expression – helplessness. He knew that feeling. He received them, offered his compassion and guided them according to the needs – some to the emergency ward, some to the Covid ward, some for documentation. He would stay with them till the time they knew that they were being appropriately attended to.

The sight of a hospital can be intimidating for the poor. They cannot read signs; they are too nervous to ask for help and almost everyone else appears to be superior to them. Sunil Paswan knew this feeling.

He was so good at guiding the swarm of patients and their anxiety ridden family members as they came face-to-face with the cold edifice of the hospital, that soon he became the Man Friday of the hospital administration. More than anything else Covid hospitals had become a centre of chaos for the sheer scale of guess work it entailed in managing the health crises. Doctors did not know what to do, what to prescribe, the nurses did not know what to say, how to act, the support staff did not know where to guide and where to shoo. A system designed and dependent on an elaborate labyrinth of orders can freeze in the face of ambiguity of this scale. However, institutions run on pretences more than real action – and in this particular case, the pretence of control had still been upheld. It was tragic.

It was also the perfect condition for someone like Sunil Paswan to take over. He had taken over the chaos, and in his own rustic style converted that chaos into an order that only keen life-long students of human chaos could create. Education and its grand edifice is singularly incapable of teaching this – only life can.

The chaos of the hospital, more than anything else, is an unruly manifestation of the chaos of an anxious human mind. There is no pattern in it. It is erratic. There is no linearity of cause and effect.

There was a reason why it required someone like Sunil Paswan to tame it. He had grown with such little order in his circumstances, that he was at home with chaos. It was order which he always struggled with. Amidst chaos, he was at home, at Ara in Bihar.

As he dealt with the madness in the hospital, he rubbed off this calm and order to others and got recognised for it. His contributions were not of technical expertise, but of something that could only be experienced. Institutions and life are indebted to those who do the immeasurable and the intangible.

Sunil experienced an amazing peace within himself. As a gateman he was also at home. In giving directions to the sick, the afraid, the fearful and the hopeless, he made a grand meaning out of his ordinary life. For the first time in his life, no one asked him his caste, his education – no one asked him his competence to do the job. His presence itself was significant enough. It was making a difference to the people and to the situation. Nothing could have been more satisfying to the man who had shouldered the heavy burden of insignificance on his soul all his life.

In those days, amidst that chaos, directing those patients to safety and comfort, Sunil Paswan finally became the darling of his own eyes, the beloved of his own soul. There was no way he would leave this, and so even while his other friends left for their homes, he continued.

There is no good time to die. However, if at all there is a time to depart, then it is the moment when you feel significant enough in the scheme of things, when you rejoice in the look in the eyes of fellow men which says – 'You have made a difference, you have made things better, you have made me happy'. In that sense, Sunil met his death just when he was experiencing that look in the eyes of his fellow human beings for the first time in his life. On Independence Day of that year Sunil Paswan died. The circumstances of his death were no less ironic than the life of Sunil Paswan.

Sunil had escaped the rabid violence of fellow human beings, used as a weapon of superiority. He had struggled to run away from the wide chasm of a thousand-year-old phenomena. He thought he had escaped it. Even the wise Sunil Paswan did not realise that, *what we run away from, runs within us.*

The circumstances of his death were ironic as much as they were tragic. A patient had died in the hospital. The family members were emotionally volatile. Soon a large crowd gathered to protest against the doctors, staff and the hospital. No one remembers exactly if the cause of death was negligence or not – who has the time check facts in these volatile times? Doctors and healthcare workers are angels of hope when everything is fine and become the subject of public ire when things don't go well. They live condemned lives – those whom they serve selflessly turn against them.

All protests begin with an individual complaint – then layers get added and it becomes a monster.

The protestors agitating against the doctors became bigger. It became a protest by the poor. Soon some local politician jumped into it and a service deficit issue, which had become a class disparity issue, became a caste discrimination issue. Violence multiplied. Vehicles were burnt, tear gas shells were fired and the police lathi charged. The crowd swelled further and as a last resort, the police opened fired at the mob.

In that melee, a rogue bullet hit Sunil Paswan, who in that moment was at his heroic best, trying to control the mob, and help the injured. Just because it was a rogue bullet that did not mean it did not know how to do its job. It killed Sunil Paswan.

If Sunil Paswan had known the name of the patient whose death had sparked the protests, he would not have been as proud of his death as he was in his last moments. Thank God he did not know that the patient's name was Raghu Paswan.

ACKNOWLEDGEMENTS

What are we but the prison of characters and stories! Each of the stories and characters within us need an escape. This book finally offers many of my stories and characters the liberation that they had been seeking for many years. Others shall continue to live condemned until another story comes along.

This book brewed for many years without any sign of itself and then suddenly it appeared. The mayhem of Covid-19 provided the necessary turmoil for it to break free. A large part of the material of the book was written much before Covid-19 and so it had to be repurposed to tell the tale. The repurposing was experimental, while the writing was therapeutic.

I lost my Dad to the virus almost around the same time I submitted the manuscript to the publisher. I am proud of the book, but I often agonise that I paid an exorbitant price for the story. I wish I could let the story go and get Dad back.

I must thank many who have been fellow travellers during this journey.

Gurbani, Keerat, Anu – I take time from you for granted. Wish I knew how to balance my time better.

Priya and Ranjita – Thank you for being a part of my life with the adulation that I often feel is misplaced.

I did an informal concept testing of the book with many, but the one who participated in it with a pleasant and surprising alacrity and in many ways became the accidental first editor was, Bijal – thank you for your effort.

Finally, everything begins somewhere. A final word of gratitude yet again must go to Jhinkpani, where it all began.

- Gurucharan S Gandhi